HAMLET

PRINCE OF DENMARK

Other Works by Christopher Andrews

NOVELS

Pandora's Game
Dream Parlor
Paranormals

COLLECTIONS

The Darkness Within

SCREENPLAYS

Thirst
Dream Parlor
(written with Jonathan Lawrence)
Mistake

THEATRICAL PLAYS

Duet

VIDEO GAMES

Bankjob

HAMLET

PRINCE OF DENMARK

A Novelization by
CHRISTOPHER ANDREWS

Adapted from the play
The Tragedy of HAMLET, Prince of Denmark
by
WILLIAM SHAKESPEARE

A Rising Star Visionary Press book
for extra copies please contact by e-mail at
risingstarvisionarypress@earthlink.net
or send by regular mail to
Rising Star Visionary Press
Copies Department
P O Box 9226
Fountain Valley, CA 92728-9226

For my mother, who couldn't understand Shakespeare.

For Yvonne, my wife, editor, and Imzadi.

Thanks to
Pastor Charles Ragland and Ms. Barbara Wallis,
two "laymen" whose feedback was most appreciated.

And special thanks to
J. Max Burnett,
who cast me in the role of Hamlet in the
1992 University of Oklahoma production of
Rosencrantz & Guildenstern Are Dead,
and thereby set me upon this journey.

WHY NOVELIZE *HAMLET*?
A FOREWORD BY THE AUTHOR

I had many reasons for wanting to write a novelization of *Hamlet*, but the simplest reason was this:

For my mother. And people like her.

In 1992, while pursuing my theatre degree from the University of Oklahoma, I was cast in the role of Hamlet in Tom Stoppard's *Rosencrantz and Guildenstern Are Dead*. For those unfamiliar with this genius stage play, Stoppard took two relatively minor characters from Shakespeare's *Hamlet* and told the story of the Melancholy Dane from *their* point-of-view. The audience is given a glimpse of what went on "behind the scenes," so to speak. As one would expect, this offered a very different perspective on the Prince of Denmark.

Needless to say, I wanted my parents to be as familiar with *Hamlet* as possible before coming to see the show, so that they might understand and appreciate all of Stoppard's brilliant nuances. I called my mother and advised that she pick up a copy of one of the Hamlet movies – Mel Gibson's being the most recent version at the time, I suggested that it would be the easiest to find.

"No, I can't do that," she said.

"What do you mean?" I asked. "Mom, you *really* need to watch 'Hamlet' before coming to see this show."

"I can't," she insisted, "I've always *wanted* to watch

'Hamlet,' but I just can't understand what they're saying. I can't understand Shakespeare."

What ended up happening was that I had to rent the movie myself, drive it to my parents' house, and "translate" the whole movie for them.

The interesting thing was, as the movie played on, I had to do it less and less. They started "getting it" more and more on their own. Once she'd gotten past the difficulty – and *intimidation* – of understanding Shakespeare's text, my mother thoroughly enjoyed the story, and both of my parents appreciated *Rosencrantz & Guildenstern Are Dead* that much more.

But the whole experience got me to thinking: How many people like my mother are out there? How many people would relish Shakespeare's works, if only they had *a little help* following the dialogue?

And don't get me wrong – I remember what it was like. Before I had taken so many Shakespeare-oriented classes at the University, I often could not make heads-or-tails of *Hamlet* ... or *Macbeth* or *Julius Caesar* and so on.

Too many of us only know Shakespeare from Junior High or High School English classes, and therein lies the heart the problem: Most English teachers assign *Hamlet* and other plays to be read as though they were a novel or essay. The fact is, *no* plays are meant to be read – they are meant to be *performed*. Some, more enlightened school teachers have the class read the plays aloud, which inevitably leads to far more "Ah-ha!" moments for their struggling students.

And so, my plan for novelizing *Hamlet* began to take form on two levels:

(1) I would "translate" the language, though not as

blatantly as I did for my parents back in college. I would just ... "nudge" the words a bit. Sometimes I had to alter archaic terms simply because their original syntax had changed so drastically in the modern age. A few passages required additional text to identify what could easily be called "jargon" from professions that were more commonplace in Shakespeare's time; likewise, myths and folklore that was common knowledge to the man on the streets all those centuries ago required a touch more back-story or explanation for the current reader.

But just as often, I found that simply flipping the subject/verb agreement, or reversing what *now* seems like a misplaced modifier, was often all that was needed to make the phrase or passage clear. And more than once, lines of text required no alteration at all – once the lines immediately preceding and following were clarified, the interjection made perfect sense with no help from me.

(It is also important to note that, whenever the lines are considered "poetry" or "dialogue" or "song" *within the context of the story*, I left those alone as well. When The Player recites his monologue, when Ophelia sings her song, and so on ... even in Hamlet's "world," these passages are being rendered as third-party material by the characters themselves – it's not Shakespeare the playwright "talking to the audience," per se, but Ophelia the character singing a song to those around her. And so, I left these passages as they were.)

(2) I would elaborate in the prose as to what each character (actor) might have been doing/thinking/feeling at any given point. And thus, the dialogue would become more clear, as the reader would have a greater sense of context.

For example, when it came to the Hamlet's "performance," sometimes I borrowed from Mel Gibson, sometimes I borrowed from Kenneth Branagh, and sometimes I came up with something completely (to the best of my knowledge) original.

And that's my point: *It's all a matter of interpretation.* There are no (well, few) absolutes when it comes to what a character meant or how a certain line should be delivered. Each actor brings something new; each director has their own vision. And so, by "acting out the story," I hope to give the reader a taste of what it would be like to actually *see* the play performed, and therefore better understand – and enjoy – the experience. After all, not many of us live within easy reach of the Royal Shakespeare Company.

That pretty much sums up my intentions behind this novelization. Do I hope pleasure-readers will find it more accessible now? Yes! Do I hope that perhaps students – especially those non-theatre majors – might be able to use this text as a learning aide? Sure!

So here it is. My interpretation of *Hamlet, Prince of Denmark.* I hope you find the Bard's text easier to understand, but at the same time, I *am* asking you to "put your Thinking Caps on." After all, this is still Shakespeare; I'm just hoping to sit alongside you as I did my parents all those years ago, and help you understand the story that much better. I've tweaked, I've rearranged, I've converted ... but *whenever* possible, I've left things as unaltered as I could.

And there are certain phrases that simply *demanded* to be left alone:

To thine own self be true.

Frailty, thy name is woman.

To be or not to be? That is the question.
Some lines just *had* to stay.
Enjoy!

Christopher Andrews
June, 2005

DRAMATIS PERSONAE

HAMLET, Prince of Denmark, son to the late King, and nephew to the present King

CLAUDIUS, the new King of Denmark, Hamlet's uncle

THE GHOST of the late King Hamlet, Prince Hamlet's father

GERTRUDE, the Queen, Hamlet's mother, now wife of Claudius

POLONIUS, Lord Chamberlain, councillor of the State of Denmark

LAERTES, Polonius' son

OPHELIA, Polonius' daughter

HORATIO, true friend and confidant of Hamlet

ROSENCRANTZ
                  } courtiers, former schoolfellows of Hamlet
GUILDENSTERN

FORTINBRAS, Prince of Norway

VOLTEMAND
                  } Danish councillors, ambassadors to Norway
CORNELIUS

MARCELLUS, a Danish officer

BERNARDO
} Members of the King's guard on sentry duty
FRANCISCO

OSRIC, a foppish courier

REYNALDO, servant to Polonius

THE PLAYERS, an acting troupe

A GENTLEMAN of the court

A PRIEST

1ST RUSTIC, a grave-digger

2ND RUSTIC, the grave-digger's companion

A NORWEGIAN CAPTAIN in Fortinbras' army

ENGLISH AMBASSADORS

LORDS, LADIES, SOLDIERS, SAILORS, MESSENGERS, and ATTENDANTS

LOCATION

DENMARK, the ROYAL CASTLE OF ELSINORE, and its environs

PART ONE
CHAPTER ONE

The frigid night air cut Bernardo to the bone.

He hastened his stride in a vain effort to warm himself. The mist was heavy, dampening his clothing and making him feel colder still. He always dreaded these nighttime shifts guarding the platform of the castle of Denmark's Elsinore, and the bizarre occurrences of the past two nights did nothing to improve his disposition. The echo of his boots against the stone surface made his footsteps sound uncomfortably like a quickened heartbeat, giving him cause to shudder that had nothing to do with the chilled air. Still, the hour drew late, and Francisco required relief; one man could not guard the platform all night.

As he rounded a parapet, he caught a glimpse of movement within the shadows, bringing his step, and his breath, to a sharp pause. All things being equal, he knew it must be Francisco ... but of late, all things were *not* equal.

"Who's there?" he demanded, his hand drifting down to the hilt of his sword.

"Nay, *you* answer *me*!" came the expected – and therefore relieving – response. "Halt and identify yourself!"

Bernardo smiled. "Long live the King!"

"Bernardo?"

"Aye, it's me," Bernardo reassured him. He advanced to join his fellow sentinel upon the upper portion of the platform.

Francisco breathed his own sigh of relief. "You have arrived quite promptly for your duty."

"The time is midnight," Bernardo said, clapping him on the shoulder. "Get yourself to bed, Francisco."

Francisco smiled, an expression barely visible in the dark of the night. "Much thanks for the relief. It is bitter cold, and my spirits are low."

Bernardo nodded in understanding. He wished *he* were the one going off watch rather than just starting. "Have you had a quiet night?"

"Not a mouse stirring."

"Well, good night. If you see Horatio and Marcellus, my partners on this watch, ask them to make haste."

"I think I hear them," Francisco told him, peering into the shadows from which Bernardo had just emerged. Bernardo followed his gaze. Two figures slowly became visible as they approached.

"Halt!" Francisco called out. "Who is there?"

"Allies of this land," came Horatio's familiar voice.

Immediately after drifted Marcellus', "And loyal subjects to the King of Denmark."

Satisfied, Francisco strode forward, speaking as he passed them. "God give you a good night."

"Oh, farewell, honest soldier," Marcellus returned. "Who relieved you?"

"Bernardo took my place," he said, then repeated, "God give you a good night." And with that, Francisco was gone.

"Hello, Bernardo," Marcellus greeted him as he and his companion joined the sentinel at his post.

"Is this Horatio with you?" Bernardo asked.

"Oh," Horatio answered with a short chuckle, "someone like him."

"Welcome, Horatio. Welcome, good Marcellus."

Horatio nodded in greeting, then cut back to his chiding. "What, has this thing appeared again tonight?"

Bernardo shook his head. "I have seen nothing," he answered in all seriousness.

Marcellus cleared his throat briefly. "Horatio says it is nothing but our *imagination*, and will not believe in this dreaded sight that we have seen *twice*. Therefore, I have convinced him to come along with us to watch the minutes of this night, so that if this apparition again comes, he may pay witness and speak to it."

Horatio chuckled again, a grin gracing his round face. He waved them away and ran his fingers through his short brown hair. "Tush, tush, it will not appear."

Bernardo stood straighter. "Sit down a while, and let us again tell you, who are so determined not to believe us, about what we have seen these past two nights."

Horatio threw his hands up in the air and sighed. "Very well, let us sit down and hear Bernardo tell his tale."

The three men gathered along a bench against the castle wall. Bernardo began, pointing upward, "Last night, when that star had reached the same point where it is now, Marcellus and I, just after the bell struck one—"

Marcellus suddenly shot his hand up, his eyes cast over Horatio's shoulder. Bernardo froze. "Please, be quiet," Marcellus whispered. "Look what comes again."

Horatio stared at him in confusion for a moment, waiting for him to speak further, then followed his gaze.

Across the platform, the shadows brightened with an

unusual light that looked like neither the sun nor a burning torch. In fact, as Horatio continued to study the peculiar sight, he found that it wasn't as if the darkness were being lighted from an external source so much as the dim seemed to simply grow *less* dim, as if by black magic. Despite the cold, he felt a sheen of perspiration forming upon his body.

"In the same image," Bernardo observed in a hushed voice, "like the late King."

From amidst the unearthly glow appeared a figure fully clad in armor. *Royal* armor. The person might have seemed normal, except for the fact that if Horatio narrowed his eyes and stared intently enough, he realized that he could just barely see *through* the image to the far wall of the castle.

"You are a scholar," Marcellus said to Horatio, "speak to it."

"Does it not look like the late King?" Bernardo insisted. "*Look* at it, Horatio."

Horatio did so, and despite the spectral nature of this phantom, he could not deny the familiarity of that wise, bearded face ... a face he had never expected to see animate again. Not in *this* life. It did indeed appear to be the recently deceased King Hamlet.

"Very much like him," Horatio agreed, his voice catching in his throat. "It harrows me with fear and wonder."

"It must be spoken to before it can speak," Bernardo murmured.

"Speak to it, Horatio."

Horatio swallowed hard against his fear and rose to his feet. The apparition moved toward them slowly, and was still a good distance away. Horatio took two steps toward it, and could make himself move no closer.

"What are you," he called with false bravado, "that invades our realm this time of night, wearing the face, and the armor in which our buried majesty, the late King of Denmark, did formerly march?" He paused, but the phantom did not respond, except to come to a halt and frown at him with eyes that were terribly frightening because they looked so real, so *alive*. "By Heaven, I charge thee speak!"

With that, the apparition turned quickly and strode away from the three men.

"It is offended," Marcellus proclaimed.

"See," Bernardo chimed in, "it stalks away."

His fear momentarily pushed aside, Horatio took a few more steps toward the retreating form. "Stay!" he called. "Speak, speak, I charge thee *speak*!"

A moment passed, then the strange glow collapsed around the figure, and in a breath ... it had vanished.

"It is gone, and will not answer," Marcellus observed.

Horatio continued to stare after the dissipated figure, unsure for what he waited. The sheen of sweat that had covered his body upon the ghost's first appearance had thickened considerably.

"How now, Horatio?" Bernardo spoke with a touch of humor, and vindication, in his voice. "You tremble and look pale. Is that not something *more* than imagination? What do you think of it?"

"Before God," Horatio declared, "I would not have believed had I not seen it with my own eyes."

Not quite as adjusted to the sight as his friend Bernardo, Marcellus paced around them, casting his gaze into the darkness as if expecting the ghost to reappear at any moment. "Is it not like the King?"

Horatio nodded. "As much as you are like yourself. So was the armor like he wore when he battled the ambitious King of Norway. His expression was like that when he defeated the Pollacks on the ice." He breathed deep. "It is very strange."

Marcellus continued to pace. "Twice before, at precisely this hour, it marched this very path by our watch."

"While I have no precise theory to explain this," Horatio told his companions, his fingers running through his hair again, "my feeling is that this bodes some strange trouble within our lands."

Marcellus, finally satisfied that they were again alone, gestured back toward the bench. "Come now, sit down." He paused briefly as Bernardo and Horatio joined him, then turned toward the latter. "Tell me, as you would know, why we have kept this same strict watch, and why we daily deal with the foreign market for weapons of war, why we force service of shipwrights, who are made to work every day of the week, even Sunday. What might be in preparation, that this sweaty haste makes us all work day and night? Can you inform me?"

"That I can, at least as far as the rumors go," Horatio answered him. Bernardo and Marcellus leaned closer as he continued. "Our late King Hamlet, whose image even now appeared to us, was, as you know, challenged to combat by his rival, King Fortinbras of Norway. If our valiant Hamlet slew Fortinbras, by sealed agreement honored by heraldic law, he forfeited with his life all those lands which he possessed – not his kingdom, but his personal lands – to the conqueror. An equivalent portion was pledged by *our* King, which would have been relinquished to Fortinbras had *he* been the vanquisher. By the agreement made, Fortinbras lost his lands to King Hamlet." Horatio's heart swelled with pride at the victory of his late liege, then he pressed on. "Now, *young* Fortinbras, full of hot, untried mettle, has hastily gathered up from the outlying territories of Norway a list of lawless ruffians for some bold enterprise, which we believe is to take back his father's lands *by force*. This, I take it, is the primary motivation for our preparations, the reason for this very watch, and the chief source of this posthaste bustling activity in the land."

Bernardo cleared his throat. "I think there can be no other reason. It fits well that this ominous figure comes armed through our watch so like the King that was and is the question of these wars."

Horatio agreed, "It is a mote of dust to trouble the mind's eye. In the most high and flourishing sovereignty of Rome, a little before the mighty Julius Caesar fell, the graves stood open and the recently dead appeared in the Roman streets. Astounding sights filled the elements, such as falling stars and dews of blood, ominous signs in the sun and in the moon, upon whose influence Neptune's sea was almost totally darkened. And similar foreshadowing of feared events – as advanced warning of things to come – have Heaven and Earth manifested upon our regions and countrymen."

As Horatio spoke, his gaze drifted back to the area from which the ghost had emerged. With a start he realized that the apparition had reappeared, and was now closer to them than it had been before. He drew a breath and whispered sharply, "Quietly, behold! It comes again!"

The three shot to their feet. As the ghost approached

them, it slowly spread its arms, causing Horatio's blood to run like ice through his veins. He wanted nothing more than to retreat, to run from this place and never return, but he knew that his duty demanded much more.

Steeling himself, he moved to intercept the silent, frightening phantom. *I shall cross its path and confront it directly, though it may wither me.* He called, "Stay, illusion!" The image again frowned upon him, but continued to advance slowly as Horatio and his companions made an equally lingering withdrawal. "If you have any sound or use of voice, speak to me. If there is any good thing to be done that may ease you, and grace me, speak to me. If you are privy to your country's fate, which forewarning might help us *avoid*, speak!" The ghost still made no reply, and Horatio's voice grew more bold. "Or if thou hast, in thy life, hoarded extorted treasure in the womb of the earth, for which, they say, your spirits often walk in death, speak of it, stay and *speak*!"

At that moment, from a pier to their left, a rooster crowed into the night. The ghost started visibly, almost as if in pain, and began retreating once more.

Desperate to find some answers, Horatio ordered, "Stop it, Marcellus."

Marcellus looked at him as if he had gone mad. "Shall I strike it with my spear?"

"Do it, if it will not be still."

Reluctantly, Marcellus brandished his weapon, and the three men strode after it. They rounded a corner, and for a moment thought they had lost it. Bernardo pointed toward where it now walked, an impossible distance away. "There it is!"

They ran further, but the ghost managed to stay ahead of them. Horatio pointed as it seemed to come to a halt. "There it is!"

Marcellus drew back his arm to cast the spear, but it was too late. The strange glow again enveloped the ghost, and it vanished for the second time.

"It is gone!" Marcellus lowered his spear in frustration. "We did it wrong," he said to Horatio, "to offer it the show of violence, for it is as the air, invulnerable, and our vain gestures were empty pretenses."

Bernardo, out of breath from their spontaneous run, observed, "It was about to speak when the rooster cried."

"And then it started like a guilty thing upon a fearful summons," Horatio added. "I have heard that the cock, the trumpeter of morning, awakens the god of day with his lofty and shrill-sounding throat, and at its crow – whether in sea or fire, in earth or air – the spirits of the dead must hastily return to their confines. This present sight proves it is true."

Marcellus nodded, slowly at first then with intensity. "It faded on the crowing of the cock," he agreed. "Some say that by the time that season comes wherein our Savior's birth is celebrated, the bird of dawning sings *all* night long. And then, they say, no spirit *dares* stir abroad; the nights are wholesome; then no malicious planetary alignments strike, no fairy bewitches, nor witch has power to charm, so hallowed and so *good* is the time."

Never the superstitious but ever the diplomat, Horatio merely said, "So have I heard, and do – in part – believe it." He grit his teeth and once more ran his fingers through his hair. "Look, morning lies just beyond that eastern sky. We must break our watch, and I suggest that we tell young

Hamlet of what we have seen tonight, for, upon my life, this spirit, mute to us, will speak to him. Do you agree that we must inform him, as much for love as for duty?"

Bernardo and Marcellus both nodded in agreement. Marcellus spoke, "Let us do it, and I know where we will find him this morning ..."

The three made their plans as the freezing night listened in silence.

PART ONE
CHAPTER TWO

A flourish of trumpets echoed throughout the room of state at Elsinore. The Lord Chamberlain Polonius gestured, and the members of the royal council of Denmark, as well as the small audience – which included the Chamberlain's son, Laertes – bowed their heads and knelt to one knee, followed a moment later by Polonius himself. The chamber doors opened, and Claudius, the new King of Denmark, entered the room. He paused at the entrance, allowing his royal visage to bathe his congregation for a few moments. He then reached out to his left, his palm open in expectation, and Queen Gertrude appeared to take his hand in her own. With his new bride at his side, Claudius ascended the dais to his throne. The Queen took her seat, and then the King lowered himself. He waited a moment longer, then clapped his hands sharply. The assembly rose to their feet, and Claudius beamed openly as they again nodded their heads before his majesty.

From the rear of the state room, seated upon steps leading to another level of the chamber and shrouded in shadow, young Hamlet, the Prince of Denmark, watched the proceedings. He did not bow, nor did he lower his head. He merely sat and watched ...

... and brooded.

The King hesitated in what young Hamlet was sure he perceived as dramatic pause, then addressed the throng.

"Though the memory of dear brother Hamlet's death

may yet be fresh," he spoke, his baritone voice carrying more efficiently through the room than Prince Hamlet would have preferred, "and it would benefit us to bear grief in our hearts, and our whole kingdom to be reduced to one mournful brow ... *discretion* demands that we think of him, as well as *ourselves*. Therefore, with an impaired joy, with one eye cheerful and the other weeping, with laughter in funeral and with dirge in marriage, weighing equally delight and grief ... with all this, I have taken my former sister-in-law – the Queen, the imperial joint-holder to this warlike state – as my *wife*. You have, in good wisdom, condoned this fully and without reservation. For all this, I give my thanks."

The audience applauded. From his viewpoint in the shadows, Hamlet realized that he had unconsciously clenched his fist until finally his fingernails threatened to break through the skin of his palm. He made a half-hearted attempt to calm himself.

"I must next inform you," Claudius continued, rising to his feet and pacing slowly before the throne, "that young Fortinbras, holding a weak opinion of our worth, or thinking my late dear brother's death has left our state disjointed and out of frame, has contrived with this false dream to take the advantage – he has assailed me with persistent messages demanding the surrender of those lands lost by his father, lost with all binding terms of the *law*, to my most valiant, late brother, King Hamlet." Claudius halted his easy stride and smiled over his shoulder to the congregation. "So much for him."

His listeners laughed. All save one.

"Now for ourselves," the King recommenced, returning once more to the throne, "and for this meeting, this is our business: We have written to Norway, the uncle of young Fortinbras – who, feeble and bedridden, barely hears of his nephew's purpose – to suppress his further proceeding herein, as the monies, the soldiers, and the full supplies are all drawn from the liegemen of Norway. We now dispatch you, good Cornelius, and you, Voltemand ..." The two men stepped forward from the collective body. "To bear this greeting to old Norway, giving you no more personal power in your business with the King than the range that these detailed articles allow."

From within the folds of his cloak, Claudius produced a scroll, fastened with his royal seal. Cornelius, his back straight and his head high, marched up the steps and took the paper from the King's hand with an overly-sharp bow of his head. He then descended to again stand beside his fellow herald.

"Farewell," Claudius told them, "and let haste command your duty."

Cornelius and Voltemand spoke in unison. "In that, and all things, will we show our duty."

Claudius seemed to find their uniform performance somewhat amusing, and his tone was light as he returned, "I doubt it not at all; heartily farewell."

The heralds effected a snap-turn to the right, and marched from the state room. Hamlet eyed them with vague repugnance as they departed.

"And now, Laertes," the King addressed the Lord Chamberlain's son, "what's the news with you? You told us of some entreaty – what is it, Laertes?"

The Chamberlain's son stepped forward, then seemed to grow nervous and lose his words.

Claudius chuckled. "You cannot speak reasonably to the King of Denmark and waste your voice. What would you ask, Laertes, that I shall not offer? The head is not more closely related to the heart, the hand more instrumental to the mouth, than is the throne of Denmark to your father." Lord Chamberlain Polonius modestly averted his eyes at the compliment. "What would you have, Laertes?"

Laertes took another step forward. "Your gracious permission to return to France, my revered lord, from where, though I willingly came to Denmark to show my duty in your coronation ... I must now confess, that duty done, my thoughts and wishes bend again toward France, and I request your gracious permission to depart." He bowed deeply, as if to physically manifest his sincerity.

Claudius seemed to ponder his decision for the briefest of moments. "Have you your father's leave? What says Polonius?"

The Lord Chamberlain spoke, and there was a degree of humor in his voice. "He has, my lord – by laborsome petition – wrung from me my slow leave, and at last upon his will I gave my reluctant consent. I do beseech you give him leave to go."

The King nodded. "Take your fair hour, Laertes – time be yours, and your best virtues spend it at your will!"

Laertes smiled from ear to ear and rejoined his father.

Claudius returned the young man's glow, then his expression grew more somber. He rose again to his feet, and glanced toward his wife. She nodded, her own face a mask of concern, and followed him as he descended the steps. The audience, slightly taken aback, scrambled as graciously as they could to part for their monarch. Prince Hamlet realized too late what was transpiring, and cursed himself for not retreating from sight when he had the chance.

"But now," Claudius picked up as though he had never stopped speaking, "my nephew Hamlet, and my son ..."

A little closer than a nephew, Hamlet spat to himself, *as you are my mother's husband, and my father's brother ... but I am* not *your son.*

"... how is it that the clouds still hang on you?"

Hamlet regarded the King, and purposely did not stand when he answered, "Not so, my lord, I am *too much* in the sun."

Claudius blinked, and for an instant, Hamlet thought he glimpsed a flash of irritation behind the sovereign's eyes. The idea brought him more than a little satisfaction.

"Good Hamlet," Queen Gertrude, his mother, interjected, "cast your darkened color off, and let your eye look friendly on Denmark. Do not search forever with downcast eyes for your noble father in the dust. You know it is universal – all that lives must die, passing through nature to eternity."

Hamlet looked away from his mother. "Aye, madam, it is universal."

"If it is, why does it seem so *personal* with you?"

Hamlet's gaze now snapped to her, and Gertrude was taken aback by the anger and hurt she saw in her son's countenance. " '*Seems*,' madam? No, it *is* – I know not 'seems.' It is not only my inky cloak, good mother, nor customary suits of solemn black, nor forced sighing, nor the plentiful tears in the eye, nor the dejected behavior of the visage. *Together*, with all forms, moods, shapes of grief, can truly portray my feelings. These indeed 'seem,' for they are actions that a man might pretend, but I feel them and show them with *sincerity*."

"It is sweet and commendable in your nature, Hamlet," Claudius said to him, and Hamlet only resisted striking out at him with firm resolve, "to give these mourning duties to your father. But you must know your father lost a father, that father lost his, and the survivor always mourned for a time." His tone then darkened. "But to *continually* mourn is blasphemous *stubbornness* – it is unmanly grief; it shows a will unsubmissive to Heaven, an insecure heart, or impatient mind, an understanding simple and *unschooled*." Claudius straightened, and his following words were obviously intended as a show for his masses. "For what we know must be, and is as common as any of the most common experiences, why should we, in our quarrelsome opposition, take it against the heart? Fie, it is an insult to Heaven, an insult to the dead, an insult to nature, to contrary reason, whose common theme *is* death of fathers, and who still has cried, from the first corpse till he that died today, '*This must be so.*' "

Hamlet glared at Claudius. If the King noticed, he did not offer a hint as he again lowered his voice to a level that would at least *appear* to be sincere, but could still be heard by all. "Seems" indeed!

"I ask you throw this unending woe to earth, and think of *me* as a father, for let the world take note: *You* are the most immediate heir to the throne, and with no less nobility of love than that which a most loving father bears his son do *I* give to *you*." Claudius paused, perhaps hoping Hamlet would make some response – after all, he had just announced, publicly, that young Hamlet would be the next man to sit upon the throne of Denmark. When it became clear that none was forthcoming, he pressed on, a gentle hand at the small of the Queen's back. "Your intent in going back to school in Wittenberg is contrary to our desire, and we beseech you, incline you, to remain *here* in the cheer and comfort of our eye, our chiefest courtier, cousin, and our son."

This Hamlet found quite interesting. As it happened, if he had not been away at school at the time, the decision as to *who* would, in fact, succeed the deceased King might have swayed to a different breeze. And now that it mattered not ... Claudius wanted him to *stay*? All the better to keep an eye on him, most likely!

Either way, he cared little for his uncle/step-father's wishes, and might have refused then and there, had his mother not pleaded, "Do not let your mother lose her prayers, Hamlet. I beg you to stay with us – do not go to Germany."

Hamlet looked into her eyes, at the despondent look upon her face, and sighed. "I shall, in all my best, obey you, madam."

Claudius smiled broadly. "Why, it is a loving and fair reply. Be as free as us in Denmark. Madam, come." He guided his Queen away, and with a gesture, dismissed the assembly as well. "This gentle and unforced agreement of Hamlet warms my heart, and we shall hold a celebration that will sound through the heavens. Come away ...!"

A few minutes later, Hamlet was alone.

The Prince of Denmark regarded his cold, shadowed, empty surroundings. How they seemed to reflect the ache in his heart.

Oh, he thought, *that this too solid flesh would melt, thaw, and dissolve into a dew! Or that the Everlasting had not fixed his law against self-slaughter!* The Prince rose to his feet and paced slowly about the lonely chamber. "Oh God, God, how weary, stale, flat, and unprofitable all the customs of this world seem to me! Damn it all, *damn*!" His words echoed through the room, with no reply other than the continuation of his own thoughts. *It is an unweeded garden that grows to seed, things rank and gross in nature possessing it utterly. That it should come to this! Only two months dead ... no, not even two. So excellent a king, that was to this land as the titanic sun-god Hyperion was to a lecherous satyr, so loving to my mother that he might not allow the winds of Heaven to visit her face too roughly.* Hamlet's pacing brought him before the throne, and he sat upon the steps, his back to the exalted seat. "Heaven and Earth, must I remember? Why, she would hang on him as if her appetite would increase by what it fed on. And yet, within a month ..."

Hamlet turned and glanced up to the throne, and pictured the new king, his uncle-father, sitting upon it beside his aunt-mother. He quickly turned away, closing his eyes tightly. "Let me not think on it! Frailty, thy name is *woman*!"

His cry again rang through the assembly room, reverberating off the walls as if to mock him.

"A little month, before those shoes were old with which she followed my poor father's body, like the weeping Niobe, all tears ... why, she, even she ... oh, God, a *beast* that lacks the power of reason would have mourned longer ... she married my uncle, my father's *brother*, but no more *like* my father than I am to Hercules. Within a month, before yet the salt of most hypocritical tears had left the redness in her swollen eyes, she *married*."

Hamlet threw back his head as if to cry out in rage once more, but the words instead flowed with a defeated hush from his lips as his face came to rest in his hands. "Oh, most wicked speed. To hasten with such dexterity to those incestuous sheets, it is not, nor it cannot come to good, but *break* my *heart* ... for I must hold my tongue."

Hamlet, drowning in his sorrow as he was, failed to notice as Marcellus, Bernardo, and his close friend Horatio entered from the back of the chamber. They hesitated at the sight of their beloved Prince, and Marcellus looked to Horatio as if to question whether or not they should leave and return at a later time, but Horatio steeled himself and beckoned them forward.

"Hail to your lordship!" Horatio called.

Hamlet stirred a bit, too apathetic of the world around him to be truly startled by the disturbance. "I am glad to see you well," he mumbled in reflexive response. The Prince then looked up, and when he realized who had addressed him, his spirits lifted noticeably and he rose to his feet. "Horatio, or I do forget myself."

Horatio smiled at the positive change in his friend's poise. "The same, my lord, and ever your poor servant."

Hamlet crossed the room to meet them and locked hands with Horatio. "Sir, my good *friend*. I'll exchange *that* name with you." He smiled warmly, and for the first time since his father's death, it felt natural. "And what brings you from Wittenberg, Horatio?" The Prince then caught himself, and realized that he had completely ignored the sentinels, and also friends, who accompanied Horatio. "Marcellus," he nodded.

Marcellus returned the bow. "My good lord."

"I am very glad to see you." He nodded again, this time to Bernardo. "Good evening, sir."

Bernardo smiled and bowed from the neck as had Marcellus.

Feeling he had now at least answered courtesy's demands, Hamlet returned his focus to Horatio. "But, truly, why are you away from school?"

"An urge to play absentee, my good lord," Horatio told him with a wink.

Hamlet chuckled and shook his head. "I would not hear your enemy say so, nor shall you hurt my ears by reporting against yourself. I *know* you are not negligent. But what is your business in Elsinore? We'll teach you to drink deeply before you depart."

Horatio sighed. "My lord," he admitted, "I came to see your father's funeral."

Hamlet scoffed, "I ask you do not mock me, fellow student. I think it was to see my mother's wedding."

Horatio and his companions shuffled uncomfortably. "Indeed, my lord," Horatio agreed, unsure of how else to respond, "it did follow quickly."

"Thrift, thrift, Horatio, the funeral's cold meat pies did furnish the marriage tables. I wish I had met my most hated foe in Heaven before I had seen *that* day, Horatio!" Torn with anger and hurt, Hamlet turned away from his friends. He looked again to the throne and whispered, "My father. I think I see my father."

Much to the Prince's surprise, his words provoked a

violent response from Horatio and his companions. The sentinels looked around as if they expected an attack from every side at once, and Horatio himself drew his sword, his face pale and riddled with fear. "Where, my lord?" he demanded.

Hamlet stared at his friend, and found himself wondering if perhaps *Horatio* had been driven mad over recent events. "In my *mind's eye*, Horatio."

Horatio and the sentinels looked at one another and relaxed their stance, Marcellus and Bernardo averting their eyes in embarrassment. Horatio, however, decided this was the time. "I saw him once, he was a goodly king."

Still staring in confusion at his friend, Hamlet agreed, "He was a man – take him for all in all, I shall not look upon his like again."

Horatio swallowed hard. "My lord ... I think I saw him *last night*."

"Saw who?"

"My lord, the King, your father."

The breath draining from him, Hamlet repeated in a harsh whisper, " 'The King, my father.' "

Horatio returned his sword to its sheath and held up a hand. "Hold still your disbelief, my lord, and listen, so that I may report, upon the witness of these gentlemen, this marvelous tale to you."

Part of Hamlet knew that he should be discarding Horatio's words as madness, and quickly call to the royal guard for assistance. Instead, he remained short of breath, and commanded, "For God's love, let me hear!"

Horatio steadied himself, and began. "For two nights these gentlemen, Marcellus and Bernardo, together on their watch, in the dead waste and middle of the night, have been thus visited: A figure like your father, armed in every detail, from head to foot, appears before them, and with solemn march goes slow and stately by them. Three times he walked by their oppressed eyes within his truncheon's length, while they, turned almost to jelly in fear, stood quietly and did not speak to him. They disclosed this to me in dreadful secrecy, and I kept the third night's watch with them, where, as they had reported, every word made true and good, the apparition appeared. I *knew* your father. These hands do not resemble one another any more than the apparition resembled the former King."

"But where was this?"

Marcellus answered, "My lord, upon the platform where we watch."

"Did you not *speak* to it?" the Prince demanded.

"My lord, I did," Horatio told him, "but it made no answer. Once I thought it lifted up its head and did make a gesture as if to speak, but even then the morning cock crew loud and at the sound it shrunk away in haste and vanished from our sight."

Hamlet remained silent for a moment, his eyes alight with thought, his breath still coming in quick, excited gasps. "It is very strange."

Horatio stood tall. "As I do live, my honored lord, it is true, and we did think it was written in our duty to let you know of it."

Hamlet nodded emphatically. "Indeed, indeed, sirs. But this troubles me. Do you hold watch tonight?"

Marcellus and Bernardo answered together. "We do, my lord."

"Armed, you say?"

Again together, "Armed, my lord."

"From top to toe?"

Horatio had to repress a smile as they answered in unison a third time, "My lord, from head to foot."

"Then you did not see his face?"

"Oh, yes, my lord," Horatio quickly insisted, "he wore his visor up."

"What, he looked frowningly?"

"An expression more in sorrow than in anger."

"Pale, or red?"

"No, very pale."

Hamlet grew more and more excited as he continued. "And fixed his eyes upon you?"

"Undeviating," Horatio told him.

Hamlet began pacing again, but his manner was not depressed as before. "I wish I had been there."

"It would have amazed you."

"Very likely, very likely. Did it stay long?"

Horatio considered. "While one might count slowly to one hundred."

Marcellus and Bernardo again spoke together, insisting, "No, *longer*."

"Not when I saw it," Horatio asserted.

Hamlet pressed, "His beard was streaked with gray, no?"

"It was, as I have seen it in his life, a sable silvered."

Hamlet stopped before them, his hand coming to rest at his waist, where the hilt of his sword normally rested. "I will watch tonight – perhaps it will walk again."

"I believe it will," Horatio agreed.

"If it assumes my noble father's person," Hamlet said quietly, more to himself than to those present before him, "I'll speak to it though Hell itself should gape and bid me hold my peace." He then looked to them and said, "I ask you all, if you have thus far concealed this sight, let you continue to hold your silence, and whatever else shall happen tonight, give it due thought, but do not speak of it. I will do the same. So fare you well. Upon the platform between eleven and twelve, I'll visit you."

Now Horatio joined the sentinels in stating, "Our duty to your honor."

Hamlet returned, "Your loves, as mine to you. Farewell."

The three men turned and marched from the room, and Hamlet again found himself alone. This time, his tone was different as his voice echoed from the stone walls. "My father's spirit ... in arms! All is not well – I suspect some foul play. If only the night were here! Until then, sit still, my soul. Foul deeds will rise, though all the Earth overwhelm them, to men's eyes."

Hamlet stood facing the throne, unaware that his hand again searched for the hilt of his sword.

PART ONE
CHAPTER THREE

In the Lord Chamberlain's quarters, a scant hundred yards from where Hamlet stood contemplating, Laertes waited for his father and spent a last few moments with his sister, Ophelia.

"My possessions are already abroad," he told her as he hugged her briefly. "Farewell. And, sister, as the winds are favorable and the means of conveyance is available, do not sleep, until you let me hear from you."

Ophelia pouted and slapped his arm, although Laertes was sure he caught a glimpse of humor in her green eyes. "Do you doubt that?"

Laertes smiled, then grew more serious. He would not see his sister again for some time, and he had sober advisement to give – he wished not to hurt her, but to *warn* her as was his brotherly duty. He brushed her dark hair back from her fair face and told her, "As for Hamlet, and the trifling of his attention, regard it as the typical behavior and idle fancy of a young man, a violet in the youth of springlike nature – precocious, not permanent; sweet, not lasting; the perfume and pastime of a minute ... nothing more."

Ophelia pulled away from him. Not every girl caught the attention of a Prince, and who was her brother to tell her to ignore it? "Nothing more than that?"

"Nothing more," Laertes insisted, "for the trials and tribulations of youth affect the *mind* and *soul* as well as the body. Perhaps he loves you now, and now no stain nor deceit can sully the virtue of his desire, but you must *beware*. His princely status considered, his fate is *not his own*, for he himself is subject to his birth. He may not indulge his own wishes, as common folk do, for the safety and health of this whole state depends on his choice ... and therefore his choice *must* be encompassed unto the voice and consent of the state whereof he is the head."

Laertes paused. Ophelia had turned away from him, but he judged from the stiffness in her posture that she still listened to him, and he continued, "Then if he says he loves you, it fits your wisdom to believe it as far as he – acting as he *must* in his role as Prince – may act upon his words ... which is no further than the collective voice of Denmark will allow. Then weigh what loss your honor may sustain if you listen naively to his songs, or lose your heart ..." He paused, cleared his throat, and forced himself to continue, "... or open your *chaste treasure* to his unrestrained longing."

With that Ophelia blushed and cast a disbelieving look upon her brother. With her reaction, Laertes also blushed, but pressed on nevertheless. "Beware, Ophelia, my dear sister, and keep your distance, out of the range and danger of desire. The most pious maid is sinful enough if she but unmasks her private beauty to the *moon* – virtue itself cannot escape defamation. Too often, the caterpillar injures the young plants of spring before their buds are opened, and in the dawn of youth, contagious pestilence are most threatening."

His tone softening, Laertes strode across the distance his sister had put between them and gently turned her toward him. He again caressed the hair from her face. "Be wary, then. Best safety lies in caution: *Youth* is often its own worst enemy."

Ophelia lowered her gaze from his and fixed it upon his chest as she spoke. "I shall keep this good lesson as a watchman over my heart." She then looked up to him once more, and he was glad to see the twinkle returned to her eyes. "But, my good brother, do not show *me* the steep and thorny way to Heaven like some clumsy pastor while *you* tread the primrose path of trifling play like a bloated and reckless lecher – be sure to heed your *own advice*."

Laertes grinned broadly and hugged her once more. "Oh, fear not for me."

Then he caught sight of movement through the doorway, and stepped away from her as Polonius rounded the far corner and headed toward his quarters. "I stay too long, here comes Father. A double blessing is a double grace – opportunity often smiles upon a second leave."

Polonius spread his arms wide and beamed at his son, halting just short of wrapping the youth in his warm embrace. "Still here, Laertes? Abroad, get abroad, for shame! The wind sits in the shoulder of your sail, and you are still here." The Lord Chamberlain took the final step forward and reached out to his Laertes. The young man bowed his head, and his father rested his palm firmly upon his scalp. "There, my blessing with thee! And remember these few words of advice: Give your thoughts no tongue, nor any unfitting thought its act. Be sociable, but by no means friendly with *every*one – those friends you have, their loyalty tested, hold *them* to your soul with hoops of steel, but do not lose your awareness of each new-hatched, immature blood. Beware of invitation to quarrel, but being in it, make your opponents beware of you. Give every man your ear, but few your voice;

listen to each man's thoughts, but reserve your judgement. Dress yourself the best you can afford, but not singular in design – rich, not gaudy, for the apparel often proclaims the man, and they in France of the best rank and station are most select and noble in that note. Be neither a borrower nor a lender, for loans often lose both themselves *and* friend, and borrowing dulls the edge of thrift."

Polonius paused, and removed his hand from his son's head. Laertes looked up but remained silent as his father took in the sight of him, and slowly placed both hands upon his shoulders. "This above all else," Polonius continued at length, "to *thine own self be true*, and it must follow, as the night the day, thou cannot then be false to any man." Then Polonius smiled, and Laertes smiled, and the mood between the two men brightened. "Farewell, may my blessing season this lesson within you."

Laertes nodded. "Most humbly do I take my leave, my lord."

"The time urges you, go, your servants wait."

Laertes nodded to his father again, then turned and hugged his sister. "Farewell, Ophelia, and remember well what I have said to you."

"It is locked in my memory," she assured him, "and you yourself shall keep the key of it."

Laertes grabbed the last of his belongings and made for the exit. "Farewell," he called, and was gone.

"What is it, Ophelia," Polonius asked, "he has said to you?"

Ophelia tensed. She recognized that tone in his father's voice, and she dreaded touching upon this subject with him. But ... what could she do but answer? "So please you," she said carefully, "something concerning the Lord Hamlet."

Polonius nodded his approval. "Indeed, well bethought. It is told to me, he has very often of late given private visits to you, and you yourself have been most free and charitable with your audience. If this is so – as it is told to me, and told cautiously – I must tell you, you do not clearly understand what is *proper* for my daughter, and for your honor. What is between you? Tell me the truth."

Ophelia bit back the angry words that strove to find their way from her lips. First her brother, now her father, treating her as if she were the youngest child who knows nothing! Still, Polonius was the Lord Chamberlain, and her father, so she simply replied, "He has, my lord, of late made many offers of his affection to me."

" 'Affection,' puh!" the Chamberlain spat, his own anger not so well hidden now. "You speak like a *young girl*, inexperienced in such perilous affairs. Do you believe his 'offers,' as you call them?"

Softly, Ophelia replied, paling before his growing onslaught, "I ... do not know *what* I should think, my lord."

"Then *I* will teach you: Think of yourself as a *baby* that has taken these offers for true payment, which they are *not*. Hold yourself more dearly, or, not to overstate the matter, you will make *me* a look like a *fool*!"

Ophelia had to bite her tongue against sharp retort, both in respect and in fear of his current mood. Here, he pretends to worry about *her* honor ... but, in truth, with her and Laertes' father, it always came back to *him*, how *he* would look, how *his* reputation would stand! Her only recourse now was to defend the honor of the sincere Prince Hamlet. "My lord, he has beseeched me with love in honorable fashion ..."

"Aye, 'fashion' you may call it. Go on, go on."

"... and has given *authority* to his words, my lord, with almost all the holy vows of Heaven."

"Aye, *snares* to catch woodcocks," Polonius scoffed. "I do know how extravagantly the soul lends the tongue vows when the blood *burns*. These blazes, Daughter, give more light than heat – you must not take them for true fire. From now on, be scantier with your maiden presence; set your visits at a higher rate than a simple *asking*. As for Prince Hamlet, believe this of him: He is young, and *he* may walk with a longer tether than may be given to *you*."

Ophelia made to look away, but her father caught her chin with his fingertips, forcing her to return his gaze.

"In short, Ophelia," he told her in a gentler but still firm tone, "do not believe his vows, for they are brokers, not of that color which their investments show, but mere agents of unholy suits, breathing like sanctified and pious vows ... the better to *deceive*. This is final and in plain terms: I will *not* have you so disgrace any momentary leisure as to give words or talk with the Lord Hamlet."

Polonius held her gaze a moment longer to ensure that his words sank into her mind, if not her heart. "Look to it, I charge you." He stepped back, drew a long breath ... then offered a half-smile, and turned to leave. "Come along."

Reluctantly, Ophelia replied, "I shall obey, my lord," and followed after her father.

PART ONE
CHAPTER FOUR

The wind gusted across the platform of Elsinore, and Horatio realized, as his ears ached and his toes grew numb, that the previous night's crispness had been a mere prologue to the chill of the season.

"The air bites wickedly," Prince Hamlet commented, almost as if he had read his friend's thoughts, "it is very cold."

Horatio agreed, "It is a nipping and sharp air."

"What hour now?"

"I think it is not quite twelve."

"No," Marcellus corrected, "twelve has struck."

"Indeed?" Horatio questioned, cursing himself for allowing the cold to so distract him. "I heard it not. It then draws near the time wherein the spirit tends to walk." At that moment, Horatio's heart leapt within his breast as a flourish of trumpets and two cannons fired, echoing off the castle walls and throughout its grounds. "What does this mean, my lord?"

Hamlet answered with a foul tone, "The King remains awake tonight and holds revels, keeps carousal, and the swaggering dance reels. And as he drains his draughts of Rhine wine down, the kettle-drum and trumpet thus cry out the triumph of his toast."

Horatio paused, gauging the Prince's mood. "Is it a custom?"

"Aye, marry, it is," Hamlet continued, his disposition,

if anything, growing darker, "but to my mind – though I am native here and born to the ritual – it is a custom more honored to *break* than to *observe*. This heavy-headed revel makes us defamed and censured by other nations, east and west. They call us drunkards, and soil our honor with the title of 'Pigs,' and indeed takes from our achievements – even those performed with excellence – the core and marrow of our reputation."

Horatio and Marcellus shifted uncomfortably before the Prince's oration, but held their tongues as he pressed on.

"So it often occurs in individual men, that for some vicious *blemish* of their nature, as in their birth – which is by no means their fault, as they cannot choose their origin – or by some *habit*, that treats the form of pleasing manners too lightly ... these men, carrying, I say, the stamp of one of these defects, either natural quality or placement of Fate, even if his *virtues* are as pure of grace as any man can possibly sustain, the vast, common opinion shall take *corruption* from that one particular fault: The smallest amount of evil, to his own shame, throws doubt upon *all* noble substance."

It pained Horatio to see his friend wrapped in such a thick shawl of misery and cynicism ... so much so that he was slow to notice the brightening of the shadows around them. By the time he looked past Marcellus, the ghostly image was closer to them than he had yet seen it.

"Look, my lord," he cried out, "it comes!"

Hamlet spun on his heel, his hand instinctively reaching for his blade, which now held its proper place at his side. His actions froze, however, when his gaze fell upon the spectral sight before him.

"Angels and ministers of grace defend us!" he sputtered

through lips that wanted nothing more than to scream. "A spirit of good, or a goblin damned, bringing the airs from Heaven, or fires of Hell, intentions wicked, or charitable, you appear in such an inviting shape that I will speak to you." He swallowed hard, taking in the armor, the visage, the eyes. "I'll call you Hamlet, King, Father, and royal Dane."

The phantom gave no reaction to his proclamation other than to pause in its stride.

"Oh, answer me!" Hamlet cried to it. "Let me not burst in ignorance, but tell why your properly rested bones, coffined in death, have broken their burial clothes; why the tomb, wherein we saw you quietly laid to rest, has opened its ponderous and marble jaws to cast you up again. What may this mean, that you, dead corpse, again in full armor revisit the glimpses of the moon, making night hideous, and we fools of the natural world so horridly to shake our disposition with thoughts beyond the reaches of our souls?" The ghost stared. "Say why is this? Wherefore? What should we do?"

For one agonizing moment longer, the ghost merely stood, rigid and unmoving, before the three men. Horatio looked to Hamlet, the spirit, then back again. Hamlet gripped the hilt of his sword so tightly that any feeling the night air had left in his fingers was now gone.

At long last, the phantom moved. It continued on its path, gesturing for Hamlet to follow.

"It beckons you to go away with it," Horatio spoke, horrified, "as if it desires some communication with you, alone."

"Look with what courteous action it waves you to a more removed ground," Marcellus whispered, "but do not go with it."

"No," Horatio agreed, "by no means."

"It will not speak," Hamlet announced, his stare never wavering from the image of his deceased father, "then I will follow it."

"Do not, my lord," Horatio insisted.

"Why, what is there to fear? I do not set my life at a trifling worth, and for my soul, what can it do to that, being a thing immortal as itself?" The ghost continued on its way, again motioning toward the Prince. "It waves me forth again, I'll follow it."

"What if it tempts you toward the water, my lord," Horatio asserted, "or to the dreadful summit of the cliff that hangs over its base into the sea, and there assumes some *other*, horrible form which might deprive you of your senses, and draw you into madness?" Hamlet seemed not to hear him as his feet began to propel him after the image, and so Horatio seized his arm. "*Think* of it! The very *place* puts ideas into every brain that looks so many fathoms to the sea and hears it roar beneath desperation, even *without* motivation."

"It waves me still," Hamlet whispered almost to himself, then called to the ghost, "Go on, I'll follow you!"

Marcellus stepped in front of the Prince and placed a firm hand upon his chest. "You shall not go, my lord."

Hamlet barked, "Unhand me."

"Heed me," Horatio also spoke in a raised voice, his grip tightening on Hamlet's arm, "you shall *not go.*"

"My fate cries out," Hamlet told them in a regal timbre, "and makes each petty artery in this body as hardy as the Nemean lion's sinew. Still I am called. Unhand me, gentlemen!"

With sudden and startling fierceness, Hamlet shook himself free of both men and drew his sword. Its blade remained low, but the action itself intimated enough of its potential.

"By Heaven," he told them in an unwavering voice, "I'll make a ghost of him that hinders me! I say away!" The two backed away from him, and he chased after the ghost just as it rounded a corner, calling out, "Go on, I'll follow you!"

Helpless, Horatio watched him disappear from sight. "He grows desperate with imagination."

Marcellus agreed. "It is therefore *not fit* to obey him. Let's follow."

"Have after. To what end will this come?"

"Something is *rotten* in the state of Denmark."

"Heaven will decide."

Marcellus looked after their Prince, then shook his head. "Nay, let's follow him."

PART ONE
CHAPTER FIVE

The Prince of Denmark felt as though his heart would break, hammering, as it was, like a madman against the cage of his breast. His mind reeled as he attempted to truly grasp what was transpiring. He had felt, upon hearing Horatio's report, that he was prepared – that he already *believed* ... but finding himself face-to-face with the spectral apparition that appeared as his late father proved almost more than he could bear.

As he rounded another twist toward the battlements of the castle platform, the warnings of his good friends finally crept their way back into the forefront of his reason, and he called out to the phantom. "Where are you leading me? Speak, I'll go no further."

At this, the ghost turned, and the facsimile of his father appeared quite content to converse here.

"*Heed my words,*" it spoke in a voice that reverberated far more than the surroundings justified.

"I will," Hamlet answered.

"*My hour is almost come,*" it said, "*when I must surrender myself to sulphurous and tormenting flames.*"

" 'To sulphurous and tormenting flames' ... alas, poor ghost!" Hamlet shivered.

"*Pity me not,*" the ghost commanded, "*but lend thy serious hearing to the tale I shall unfold before you.*"

"Speak," Hamlet whispered, "I am bound to hear."

"*So art thou to* revenge, *when thou shall hear.*"

Revenge? "What?"

"*I am thy father's spirit ...*" Again, Hamlet shuddered, and it had nothing to do with the cold, "*... doomed for a certain time to walk the night, and for the day confined to do penance in fires, til the foul sins done in my days of life are burned and purged away.*" The ghost paused, although a look of longing remained upon its face. "*If I were not forbidden to tell the secrets of my prison-house, I could unfold a tale whose lightest word would harrow up thy soul, freeze thy young blood, make thy two eyes leap from their orbits like stars, thy neatly arranged and smoothly combed locks to part, and each particular hair to stand on end, like quills upon their fearful porcupine. But this revelation of eternal affairs is not for ears of the flesh and blood. Listen, listen, oh, listen! If thou didst ever love thy dear father ...*"

"Oh, God!" Hamlet's heart ached.

"*Revenge his foul and most unnatural* murder."

"Murder!"

Murder. Hamlet's sorrow had stung deep and vast, but his sheer depression had held – his bitterness against his mother's hasty remarriage not withstanding – its deepest foundation, not simply in the unjust, wretched *unfairness* of it all, but into his burning gut that something else was amiss. Hamlet had viewed the body himself – there was no stabbing wound, no indication that his father had been slain in any conventional fashion. But to have his father taken by a *serpent*, of all things ... somehow Hamlet had never felt satisfied with that explanation. And now to learn that the fears and suspicions held deep within his soul were *true* ...

"*Murder most foul,*" the ghost continued, "*as in the best it always is, but this most foul, strange and* unnatural."

"Haste, that I may know it," Hamlet demanded, "that I, with wings as swift as thought, or the thoughts of love, may rush to my revenge."

"*I find thee* eager, *and duller shouldst thou be than the idle weed that roots itself in slothful ease on the wharf of the River of the Dead, if thou did not stir in this. Now, Hamlet, hear: It is claimed that, sleeping in my orchard, a serpent bit me ...*" Hamlet nodded his confirmation. "*... so the whole ear of Denmark is rankly deceived by false account of my death; but know, thou noble youth, the* serpent *that did sting thy father's life now wears his* crown."

Claudius! "Oh, my prophetic soul! My *uncle?*"

"Aye, *that incestuous, that adulterous* beast, *with witchcraft of his wits, with traitorous gifts – oh wicked wits and fits that have the power to so* seduce! *– won to his shameful lust the will of my most seemingly virtuous Queen.*" At this, the ghost's own feelings of torment overwhelmed its features. "*Oh, Hamlet, what a falling off there was! From* me *– whose love was of that dignity that it went hand-in-hand even with the vow I made to her in marriage – and to* decline *upon a* wretch *whose natural gifts were meager to those of* mine*! But while* virtue *will never be moved, though the lewdness courts it in angelic form ... so* lust, *though linked to a radiant angel, will satisfy itself in a celestial bed and prey on* garbage."

At last, the ghost reined in its agony of betrayal, and Hamlet realized almost absently that his own tears had joined its. The specter glanced to the east, then continued, "*But soft, methinks I sense the morning air, so let me be brief. Sleeping within my orchard – as was always my custom in the afternoon – upon my carefree hour thy uncle sneaked,* with venom of the cursed hebona, *that of yew, henbane, and ebony, in a vial, and he poured the leprous distillment in the porches of my ears, whose effect holds such an enmity with the blood of man that as swift as quicksilver it courses through the natural gates and alleys of the body, and with sudden vigor it doth* curdle – *like sour droppings into milk* – *the thin and wholesome blood. So it did to mine, and a most instant eruption formed like bark, most leper-like, with vile and loathsome crust all over my smooth body ...*"

Hamlet cringed at the memory of how his father's corpse had truly appeared – he had nearly been ill then, and felt the urge return to him briefly even now.

"*Thus was I, sleeping, by a brother's hand, all at once deprived of life, of crown, and of queen, cut off even in the blossoms of my sins, without final absolution, without spiritual preparation, and unanointed, no reckoning made, but sent to my accounting with all my imperfections in my head.*"

"Oh, horrible ..." Hamlet muttered, then with growing intensity, "oh, horrible, *most horrible!*"

The ghost stared Hamlet evenly in the eye. "*If thou hast natural feelings in thee, do not bear it, let not the royal bed of Denmark be a couch for lust and damned incest. But how-so-ever thou pursues this act, do not* taint *thy mind, nor let thy soul plot against thy* mother. *Leave her to* Heaven, *and to those thorns of guilt that prick and sting her, lodged in her bosom.*" Again the ghost regarded the eastern sky, and said, "*Fare thee well at once! The glow-worm shows the morning to be near as he begins to pale his heatless fire.*" He turned back to Hamlet and held his gaze once more as the ghostly glow began to fold in upon itself. "*Adieu,*

adieu, adieu! Remember me ..."

In a last emotional burst of desperation, Hamlet reached out to his departed father, but the figure was already gone.

A warming breeze swept past the Prince, and he found himself unsure as to whether it was in fact the approach of the morning sun ... or something otherworldly.

"Oh, all you host of Heaven!" he cried through his tight and tear-choked throat. "Oh, Earth! What else? And shall I couple *Hell*?" His body threatened to collapse beneath him, and he struck his face and thumped his chest in anger. "Oh, fie, hold, hold my heart, and you, my limbs, do not grow instantly old, but bear me stiffly up." He looked to the space where the ghost of his father stood moments before. "Remember thee! Aye, you poor ghost, while memory holds a seat in this distracted mind. Remember thee! Yes, from the writing tablet of my memory, I'll wipe away all trivial, foolish records, all wise sayings of books, all forms, all impressions of past that youth and observation has copied there, and your commandment all alone shall live within that book and volume of my brain, unmixed with lesser, baser matters. Yes, by Heaven!" He cried up into the fading night, "Oh, most noxious woman! Oh, villain, villain, smiling, damned *villain*! My memory – good it is that I write it down that one may *smile*, and *smile*, and be a *villain*! At least I am sure it may be so in Denmark."

He thrust his arms high to cry even louder, but finally his energy ebbed, and the last came out merely as a statement of inescapable oath and fact. "So, Uncle, there you are. Now to my word: It is 'Adieu, adieu! remember me.' *I have sworn it.*"

Then, the wind carried to him the voice of Horatio, its

timbre weighted with trepidation. "My lord, my lord!"

Marcellus' soon followed, "Lord Hamlet!"

Then the two men appeared before the battlement, and Horatio sighed open relief at the sight of his friend. "Heavens secure him!"

Hamlet grunted. "So be it!"

"Illo, ho, ho, my lord," Marcellus called the falconer's hunting call, also relieved but not quite as relaxed as he cast about for any sign of the ghost.

"Hillo, ho, ho, boy!" Hamlet returned with the falconer's cry. "Come, bird," he gestured them forward, "come."

With a final glance around them, the men joined their Prince upon the battlement.

"How is it, my noble lord?" Marcellus asked as they approached.

"What news, my lord?" Horatio echoed.

"Oh, wonderful!" Hamlet answered, but in a manner and with an expression that left Horatio uneasy – for despite his positive response, there was a fiery look in the Prince's eye.

"Good, my lord," Horatio said, "tell it."

Hamlet turned away, his gaze searching the night sky. "No, you will reveal it."

"Not *I*, my lord," Horatio swore, "by Heaven." He nudged Marcellus.

"Nor *I*, my lord."

"How say you then," Hamlet asked as he turned back to them, "would heart of man ever think it?" Again, that strange look in his eye. "But you'll be secret?"

"Aye," Horatio and Marcellus both pledged, "by Heaven, my lord."

Hamlet nodded and, despite their evident solitude, lowered his voice. "There's not a villain dwelling in all Denmark," he told them, "but he's a notorious *devil*."

"We need no ghost, my lord," Horatio said, "come from the grave to tell us this."

"Why, right, you are in the right ... and so, without further ceremony, I suggest we shake hands and part, you, as your business and desire shall point you, for every man has business and desire, such as it is, and for my own poor part, I will go pray."

With every syllable, Horatio's concern for his friend grew deeper still. Hamlet had not been himself since his father's death, this was true, but now his behavior seemed disjointed almost to the point of distraction. What in God's name had taken place upon this battlement?! "These are but wild and incoherent words, my lord."

"I am sorry they offend you, heartily, yes, faith, heartily."

Horatio shook his head and spoke gently, "There's no offense, my lord."

"*Yes*," Hamlet suddenly snapped back, causing Marcellus to retreat a step, "by Saint Patrick, but there *is*, Horatio, and *much* offense, too. Regarding this vision here, it is a true, honest ghost, *that* let me tell you. As for your desire to know what is between us, *conquer it* as you may. And now, good friends, as you *are* friends, scholars, and soldiers, give me one poor request."

"Whatever it is, my lord, we will."

Hamlet's voice lowered once more. "Never make known what you have seen tonight."

Horatio and Marcellus exchanged another glance, then

said together, "My lord, we will not."

But Hamlet was not satisfied. "No, but *swear* it."

"In faith, my lord," Horatio repeated, "I will not make it known."

"Nor I, my lord," Marcellus agreed, "in faith."

Still the Prince was not content. He drew his sword from his scabbard, again prompting Marcellus to take a step back. "Upon my sword."

"We have already sworn, my lord," Marcellus asserted.

Horatio nodded his agreement.

"Indeed," the curiously driven Hamlet pressed, "*upon my sword*, indeed."

Horatio opened his lips to protest the Prince's unnecessary aggression, when, from everywhere and nowhere, but if from *any*where, seemingly *beneath* them came the ghost's moan, "*Swear ...*"

Marcellus cried out.

"Ha, ha, boy," Hamlet chuckled without humor, "are you there, trusty fellow? Come on," he said to the two men, "you hear this fellow in the cellar, consent to swear."

"Propose the oath, my lord," Horatio offered hastily, his face pale and his breath short.

"Never to speak of this that you have seen, swear *by my sword*."

"*Swear ...*" the ghost's call echoed beneath them.

"*Hic et ubique?*" Hamlet continued. "Here and everywhere? Then we'll shift our ground. Come hither, gentlemen, and lay your hands upon my sword. Swear by my sword never to speak of this that you have heard."

"*Swear by his sword ...*" And now the disembodied voice was definitely coming from below.

Horatio and Marcellus stepped forward on shaky legs, placing their right hands upon the proffered hilt of the Prince's sword.

"Well said, old mole," Hamlet spoke, and not to the two men, "can you work in the earth so fast? A worthy miner! Once more, good friends."

"Oh, day and night," Horatio muttered, "but this is wondrous strange!"

"And therefore give it the courteous welcome due a stranger," Hamlet returned. "There are more things in Heaven and Earth, Horatio, than are dreamt of in man's philosophy."

And now Hamlet paused, thinking of all that he had seen and learned. It was tolerant enough to push his friends to plainly accept and be silent, but they did not know all that had been revealed to him. As much as he desired to simply descend upon his beastly, murderous uncle ... whether he liked it or not, the monster was currently accepted as the King of Denmark. He needed time to think, to plan, to plot! But how could he *possibly* act natural, knowing what he now did? How ... unless ...

Unless ... he cast to the wind all *pretense* of normality...

Aye! *There* lies the answer!

"But come," he told his eager audience, "here, as before, never, so help you mercy, however strange or odd I behave – as perchance hereafter, I shall put upon a mischievous disposition, acting like a *madman* – that you, at such times seeing me, shall *never*, with arms encumbered thus, or this headshake," Hamlet mocked folding his arms and shaking his head knowingly, "or by pronouncing of some doubtful phrase, as 'Well, well, we know,' or 'we could, if we would,' or 'if we had a mind to speak,' or 'there be, and if they might' ..."

The Prince appeared to be rambling now, his attitude almost manic, but Horatio and Marcellus said not a word to stop his flow, for his meaning was clear – he did not want his feigned condition revealed for what it was, and he would stand for no betrayal, accidental or otherwise.

"... or, such ambiguous giving out, to indicate that you know anything of me – this do swear, so grace and mercy help you at your most needful time."

Again, the ghostly voice, "*Swear* ..." although this time it seemed further away. Still, it was more than enough prompting – indeed, if they had even *needed* further motivation, which they most certainly did *not* – and they swore upon his sword.

"Rest, rest, perturbed spirit!" Hamlet called with a strained voice. Then, as he resheathed his weapon, he breathed deep of the night air, and his temper seemed to settle somewhat. Horatio silently noted that the cold no longer seemed to affect him. Perhaps this "mischievous disposition" would not be so much an act as he would have his friends believe.

"So, gentlemen," the Prince said, and his voice had also returned almost to normal, "with all my love I do commend me to you, and what so poor a man as I am may do to express my love and friendship to you, God willing, I shall not be lacking. Let us go together, and still your fingers on your lips, I pray. These times are in utter disorder. Oh, cursed spite, that ever I was born to set it right!"

Hamlet made to return to the main platform, and noticed that Horatio and Marcellus waited for their Prince to take the lead.

"Nay, come, let's go together."

Horatio and Marcellus exchanged the briefest of nervous glances, and then the three set upon their way.

PART TWO
CHAPTER ONE

Reynaldo had groaned inwardly when Polonius ordered that he should follow the Lord Chamberlain into his quarters. The pretense that the old man had offered – not that any were truly necessary, but Polonius always kept the face, if not the heart, of a gentleman – was to collect some money and letters that Reynaldo would then in turn transport to France to give to Polonius' son, Laertes.

Laertes, lucky boy that he was, had been gone only for some weeks now, but Reynaldo knew his master better than that. If Polonius did not give him some ulterior charges before he departed, then Reynaldo would eat his boots.

"Give him this money," Polonius said grandly as they entered his chambers, "and these notes, Reynaldo."

"I will, my lord," the servant said, taking the offered bag and scroll.

The Lord Chamberlain smiled, then leaned forward conspiratorially. Reynaldo swallowed back another groan – at least he was inevitably saved from tasting his own boot leather.

"You shall do marvelously wisely, good Reynaldo," he spoke in a lowered voice, "before you visit him, to make inquiries of his behavior."

"My lord, I did intend it," Reynaldo offered.

Polonius clapped his hands together twice. "Marry, well said, very well said." For a brief moment, Reynaldo actually hoped that might be the end of it, then Polonius' arm came around his shoulder as if to offer some bit of wisdom, and he knew that it was just beginning. "Look here, sir," Polonius continued, "inquire for me first what Danes are in Paris, and how, and who, what means, and where they lodge, what company, at what expense; and finding by this *roundabout* and directing of conversation that they do know my son, come you more nearer than your *direct* questions will touch it. Pretend, as it were, some distant knowledge of him, as thus, 'I know his father and his friends, and, somewhat, him.'" Polonius regarded him seriously. "Do you mark this, Reynaldo?"

"Aye," Reynaldo replied, "very well, my lord." *What I mark, dear Lord Chamberlain*, he added silently, *is that you simply want me to* spy *on your son – no more, no less.*

" 'And, somewhat, him – but,' " Polonius continued, "you may say, 'not well. But if it be he I mean, he's very wild, addicted so and so,' and there put on him what false charges you please – marry, none so *excessive* as may dishonor him, take heed of that – but such unrestrained, wild, and usual slips as are habits noted and most known to youth and liberty."

"Such as gaming, my lord."

"Aye! Or drinking, fencing, swearing, quarreling, whoring – you may go so far."

This time, it was Reynaldo who regarded Polonius. Reynaldo had always seen Polonius as a man more concerned with his self-image than anything else in the world – indeed, Reynaldo had assumed that Polonius' motive for the chore of spying was to make sure that Laertes wasn't doing anything to hurt *his* reputation abroad, if indeed he had one. But now, it seemed as though the old man *wanted* his son's name soiled. First he said not to go so far as to dishonor his son, then he wants Reynaldo to give Laertes the character of *whoring*? "My lord, *that* would dishonor him."

"Faith, *no*," Polonius gasped, waving his hands wildly, "as you may *flavor* it in the accusation: You must not put another scandal on him, that he is habitually lecherous – that's *not* my meaning. But hint his faults so artfully that they may *seem* the traits of *liberty*, the flash and outbreak of a fiery mind, a savageness in untamed blood, to which young men are generally subject."

Reynaldo wasn't buying it. "But, my good lord—"

"Wherefore should you do this?" Polonius anticipated quite incorrectly.

Sigh. "Aye, my lord, I would know that."

Polonius' hand returned to Reynaldo's shoulder. "Marry, sir, here's my drift, and I believe it is an ingenious, justifiable plan: You laying these slight blemishes on my son, as if he were a little shopworn, *mark you*, your partner in conversation, to him you would listen – if he has ever seen in the aforementioned faults of youth you hint of, be assured he confides in you as follows: 'Good, sir,' or so, or 'friend,' or 'gentlemen,' according to the phrase or the style of address of man and country."

"Very good, my lord."

"And then, sir, does 'a this - 'a does ..." A befuddled expression crosses over Polonius' face, and Reynaldo had to bite the inside of his cheek to maintain a serious demeanor. "... what was I about to say? By the mass, I was about to say something. Where did I leave off?"

"At 'confides in you as follows.' "

"At 'confides in you as follows,' Aye, marry. He

confides thus: 'I know the gentlemen. I saw him yesterday, or the other day, or then, or then, with such or such, and as you say, there he was 'gaming, there overcome by drink, there falling out at tennis,' or, perchance, 'I saw him enter such a house of sale,' namely, a brothel, or so forth." He nodded at Reynaldo knowingly. "See you now, your *bait* of falsehood takes this *carp* of truth, and thus do we of wisdom and of resourcefulness, with roundabout methods and circuitous attempts, by *indirections* find out the way things are going; so by my former lecture and advice you shall learn of my son." Polonius straightened to his full, unimpressive height, and attempted to look down his nose at Reynaldo despite the fact that he had to look *up*. The end result was quite comical. "You have understood me, have you not?"

"My lord," Reynaldo desperately assured him, "I have."

Polonius nodded sharply, pleased. "God be with you, fare ye well."

"Good my lord." Taking the bag and paper with him, Reynaldo made to retreat from the quarters.

Polonius brought him up short. "Observe his behavior *for yourself* as well."

"I shall, my lord."

"And see that he keeps up his music."

"Well, my lord."

Reynaldo waited a moment longer, to see that the speech was, in fact, over. He was rewarded with impatient expression and hand waving from the Lord Chamberlain.

"Farewell," Polonius stated coarsely.

As he finally exited the chamber, Reynaldo could no longer hold back the sigh that had been straining at his throat. Fortunately for him, even if Polonius had heard the indiscretion, he was distracted as his daughter Ophelia pushed past the servant and into the quarters. The young girl's deep distress was obvious.

"How now, Ophelia," Polonius asked instantly, "what's the matter?"

The girl ran to her father, tears barely restrained in her eyes, her hands clasping his desperately. "Oh my lord, my lord, I have been so frightened!"

"With what, in the name of God?"

Ophelia swallowed against her racing breath, forcing herself to slow down. "My lord, as I was sewing in my private room ... Lord Hamlet, with his doublet all unlaced, no hat upon his head, his stockings soiled, ungartered, and sagging down to his ankles like fetters upon a prisoner's legs, as pale as his shirt, his knees knocking each other ..." She shuddered. "... and with a look so piteous in purport as if he had been loosed out of hell to speak of horrors – he came before me."

Polonius paused for the briefest moment, then nodded knowingly. "Mad for your love?"

Ophelia paused, too, as she had not taken the time to consider this possibility. "My lord, I do not know, but truly I do fear it."

"What did he say?"

Ophelia continued speaking as she also pantomimed the apparently deranged Prince's earlier actions. Polonius' hand stroked the beard of his chin as he absorbed Ophelia's depiction. "He took me by the wrist, and held me hard, then he went to the length of all his arm, and with his other hand thus over his brow, he fell to such perusal of my face as if to draw it. He stayed so long. At last, a little shaking of mine arm, and three times his head thus waving up and down, he raised a sigh so piteous and profound as it did seem to shatter all his body and end his being. That done, he let me go, and with his head turned over his shoulder, he seemed to find his way without his eyes, for out the doors he went without their help, and to the last focused their sight upon me."

Polonius was satisfied. "Come, go with me. I will go seek the King. This is the very madness of *love*, whose violent quality destroys itself, and leads the will to desperate undertakings as often as any passions under Heaven that does afflict our natures. I am sorry – what, have you given him any hard words of late?"

"No, my good lord," Ophelia insisted, "but as you did command, I repelled his letters, and denied his access to me."

Polonius clapped his hands together sharply. "*That* has driven him mad. I am sorry that I had not observed him with better heed and judgement. I feared he did but trifle and meant to ruin you, but plague take my suspicious mind! By Heaven, it is as proper to us older folk to be over subtle in our opinions, as it is common for the younger sort to lack discretion." He took her gently by the arm and urged her forth. "Come, we go to the King. This must be known, which, being kept secret, might cause more grievous *harm* by its further concealment than *displeasure* by its revelation. Come."

Ophelia, of course, obeyed.

Rosencrantz and Guildenstern waited anxiously for the royal couple to make their appearance. While they had known young Hamlet for years, they had never before been summoned to Denmark's court here in Elsinore. People around this great state had been all prattling endlessly of the goings-on of the past months: The death of King Hamlet, the brisk and abrupt marriage of the Queen to her former brother-in-law, Claudius ...

People also spoke of Prince Hamlet, and reports abounded of his odd behavior of late. Some said that he still mourned his late father; others speculated that he had been unable to acquiesce to his mother's remarriage.

All Rosencrantz or Guildenstern knew was that Hamlet had not returned to school as planned. Horatio had been tight-lipped as always when the pair pushed him for gossip. And now this summons ...

There was nothing for them to do. The King and Queen would either appear in an instant, or they would keep the humble students waiting for hours – or days. Guildenstern stood silently off to one side of the room of state. Rosencrantz sat upon the bottom step, idly flipping a coin and muttering, "Heads ... heads ..." as he scrutinized each result.

As it turned out, their wait had finally come to an end. Both men leaped to attention as the royal cortege appeared, trumpets flourishing dramatically. The doors parted wide, and Claudius and Gertrude entered, the Queen's hand resting regally upon the King's uplifted wrist.

"Welcome, dear Rosencrantz and Guildenstern!" the King bellowed overly loud.

The pair did not react to the excessive volume. They merely bowed their respects at being acknowledged by one so high above them on the food-chain of life.

"More than our simple desire to see you once again," Claudius continued as Gertrude nodded her agreement, "the need we have to use you provoked our hasty summons. Something you have heard of Hamlet's ... 'transformation'...?"

The students exchanged a brief glance, then nodded.

"I call it so, since neither the exterior nor the inner man resembles that which it was," the King pressed on with a sad shake of his head. "What it should be, more than his father's death, that has pushed him so far from the understanding of himself, I cannot dream of." He then spread his arms, as if to embrace both men – he did not actually *touch* them, of course. "I entreat both of you that, being brought up with him from such early days – and thus so close to his youth and behavior – that you may remain in residence here in our court some little time, so that by your companionship you may draw him on to pleasures ... and to gather so much from each occasion as you may glean, what is *unknown* to us that afflicts him thus, that, once revealed, lies within our power to *remedy*."

The Queen now stepped forward to her husband's side. "Good gentlemen, Hamlet has often talked of you, and I am sure there is not living two men to whom he more adheres. If it will please you to show us so much courtesy and good will as to expend your time with us a while for the support and success of our hope ..." She glanced at Claudius meaningfully. "... your visitation shall receive such *thanks* as fits a king's *remembrance*."

Until now, both young men had been squirming inside, as the King was clearly asking them to spy upon their fellow student and friend. It was not so much loyalty as quandary that had rattled them – how does one go about surveillance upon a royal Prince?

Now, however, their choice seemed more clear. After all – when balancing the offense of a *Prince* against the gratitude of a *King* ... well, was there really a balance there at all?

Rosencrantz spoke first, "Both your Majesties might, by the sovereign power you have over us, put your dread pleasures more into *command* than to entreaty—"

Guildenstern jumped in quickly, rather than allow his foolish friend to openly admit that they, truly, had no choice in this matter. "But we both *obey*, and here given ourselves, to the utmost, to lay our service *freely* at your feet, to be commanded."

Claudius smiled openly and announced, "Thanks, Rosencrantz and Guildenstern," not realizing that his eye met each man by the incorrect name.

With the subtlety of one raised in court, Gertrude expressed her own appreciation while addressing them properly, "Thanks, Guildenstern and Rosencrantz." The King blinked, his error slowly dawning on him, but the Queen continued, "And I beseech you to instantly visit my too-much-changed son." She gestured to some of their retainers, who waited – as always – off to one side. "Go, some of you, and bring these gentlemen to where Hamlet is."

Guildenstern spoke as he gently nudged Rosencrantz toward the attendants, "Heavens make our presence and our practices pleasant and helpful to him!"

The Queen beamed. "Aye, amen!"

With that, the students were escorted away ... just as the Lord Chamberlain Polonius strode purposefully into the room.

"My good lord," he announced, taking the King to one side, "the ambassadors from Norway are joyfully returned."

Claudius beamed. "You have always been the father of good news."

Polonius preened, "Have I, my lord? I assure my good liege, I hold my duty as I hold my soul – both belong to my God and to my gracious King." He hesitated only the slightest before continuing, "And I do think, or else this brain of mine hunts not the trail of proper conduct as well as it once did, that I have found the very cause of Hamlet's lunacy."

Claudius, who had in truth only been giving the Chamberlain partial heed, snapped sharply to attention. "Oh, speak of that," the King insisted, "that do I long to hear."

Polonius, ever one to milk the most drama from any given situation, replied, "First, give admittance to the ambassadors; my news shall be the sweet dessert to that great feast."

Claudius sighed, not quite inwardly. Taking up the older man's metaphor, he allowed, "Then give grace to them, and bring them in."

Quite pleased, Polonius rushed off to summon the ambassadors.

As soon as the man retreated, Claudius gestured his wife

to his side. "He tells me, my dear Gertrude, that he has found the source of your son's illness."

Gertrude shook her head, in sadness and knowing. "I suspect it is nothing other than the main cause: His father's death ... and our overly-hasty marriage."

Claudius refused to accept guilt on that note. "Well ... we shall inquire of Polonius further ..." But his focus shifted as he spied the Chamberlain returning, ushering Voltemand and Cornelius at his side. "Welcome, my good friends! Say, Voltemand, what news from our brother Norway?"

Voltemand clicked his heels. "Most fair return of greetings and good wishes," he reported. "Upon our first broaching of the matter, he sent out to suppress his nephew's tariffs, which to him had appeared to be a preparation against the King of Poland – but, better looked into, he found it was truly against your highness. Thus offended, that his sickness, age, and impotence were so falsely deceived, he sends out arrests on young Fortinbras – which he, in brief, obeys, and receives rebuke from Norway ... and in the end makes vow before his uncle to never again give the trial of arms against your majesty. Whereon old Norway, overcome with joy, gives him three thousand crowns in annual fee, and his commission to employ those soldiers, so levied as before, against Poland. With an entreaty, herein further shown ..."

Voltemand snapped his fingers, and a small collection of papers – sealed with the crest of the King of Norway – found their way from Cornelius' hand to Voltemand's, and ultimately to Claudius'.

"... that it might please you to give quiet passage through your lands for this enterprise, on such terms of safety and provisions for Denmark as are therein set down."

Claudius accepted the papers but made no move to unseal them. Instead, he turned them over to Polonius, who swiftly tucked them into one of the many folded pockets of his robes. "It pleases us well; and at a more suitable time, we'll read, answer, and think upon this business. In the meantime, we thank you for your successful labor – go to your rest, and this evening we'll feast together. Welcome home!"

Pleased, Voltemand and Cornelius performed an about-face and strode away. Barely had their backsides cleared the exit before the royal couple descended upon their Chamberlain.

Polonius, much to their frustration – especially Gertrude's – clearly intended to proceed at his own pace. "This business is well ended. My liege, and madam, to expound what majesty should be, what *duty* is, why day is day, night is night, and time is time, were nothing but to *waste* night, day and time ..." The Queen sighed, and quite audibly. Although Polonius continued on as though he had not heard, he finally said, as though of his own accord, "*Therefore* ... since brevity is the *soul* of Wisdom, while tediousness is merely its limbs and gestures, I will be brief: Your noble son is *mad* – 'mad' I call it; for, to define true madness, what is it but to be nothing else *but* mad...? But let that go ..."

As the man threatened to veer off into yet another tangent, the Queen could remain silent no longer. "More *meaning*," she demanded firmly, "with less *rhetoric*."

Polonius, for his part, appeared sincerely offended. "Madam ... I swear I use no 'rhetoric' at all. That he is mad, 'tis true; 'tis true 'tis pity; and pity 'tis 'tis true – a foolish figure of speech ... but farewell it, for I will use no 'rhetoric.' *Mad* let us grant him, then – and now remains that we find out the *cause* of this effect ... or rather say, the cause of this *defect*, for this effect defective must have some cause ..."

Claudius and Gertrude exchanged a glance that spoke volumes: *How difficult would it prove to* replace *the Chamberlain, were they to have the old man hanged ...?!*

The meeting of eyes was not lost on Polonius, and he *tried* to press on in due haste, but the man was simply so in love with his own voice... "Thus it remains, and the remainder thus: Consider that I have a daughter – have while she is mine – who, in her duty and obedience, mark, have given me *this*!"

With clearly premeditated melodrama, the man whipped a letter from within his cavernous robes, holding it briefly high for all two of them to see. Snapping it open with a flick of his wrist, he now spoke as though *they* had been the cause for delay. "Now gather around, and surmise ..."

The King and Queen, their irritation momentarily forgotten, leaned forward.

" 'To the celestial and my soul's idol,' " Polonius read, " 'the most beautified Ophelia ...' " He paused, clucking his tongue and sending thoughts of hangings once more rushing through the Queen's mind. "That's an ill phrase, a vile phrase; 'beautified' is a *vile* phrase..." He glanced up, saw the Queen's withering gaze, and continued, "But you shall hear. Thus: 'In her excellent white bosom, these, and—' "

Now, blind to the irony of it, the Queen herself interrupted him, "This came from *Hamlet* to her?"

Polonius certainly did not appreciate how he was

pushing his luck when he chastised, "Good madam, be patient – I will be faithful." The Queen grumbled, but the King squeezed her hand to calm her. Polonius continued reading:

" 'Doubt thou the stars are fire,
Doubt that the sun doth move;
Doubt truth to be a liar;
But never doubt I love.

'Oh, dear Ophelia, I am ill-equipped to speak these words; I lack the art to count my groans ... but that I love thee best, oh most best, *believe it.* Adieu. Thine evermore most dear lady, whilst this body is to him, HAMLET.' "

Polonius frowned in clear disapproval of what he considered bad poetry, then slowly folded the letter once more. The melodrama seemed to have turned sour for him, and he spoke more sincerely than before, "*This* my daughter has obediently shown me, and more, has given *all* his letters to me, as they occurred by time, by means and place."

"But how has she *received* his love?" Claudius asked.

Again, Polonius looked offended, "What do you think of me?"

"As of a man faithful and honorable."

Polonius nodded, "I would gladly prove so. But what might you think, when I had *seen* this hot love on the wing – and I *perceived* it, I must tell you that, *before* my daughter told me – what might you, or my dear majesty your Queen here, think, if I had noted the matter in secret; or given my heart a *nap*, mute and dumb; or looked upon this love without comprehension ... what might you *think*? *No –* I went straight to work, and I addressed my little girl thus:

'Lord Hamlet is a Prince, out of your reach – this *must not be*.' And then I gave her strict orders, that she should *lock* herself from his affections, admit no messengers, receive no tokens. Which done, she took the fruits of my advice ... and he, repulsed – to make a short tale – fell into a sadness, then into a fast, then to a sleeplessness, then into a weakness, then to a lightheadedness, and ... by this descent ... into the *madness* wherein now he raves, and for which we all mourn."

Despite his claim of mutual "mourning" for the afflicted Prince, Polonius folded his arms and looked quite pleased with himself and his deduction, waiting proudly for a response.

But the King, at least, was silent for a moment, and the Queen followed his lead. All of this bizarre behavior ... over a young girl? Surely not. This "deduction" did not smack of the truth to Claudius. After all his fears of what the cause might *actually* be, this seemed somehow ... mundane. Finally, he turned to his wife, "Do *you* think it's this?"

"It *may* be, very likely." But despite her words, *she* didn't sound convinced, either.

In fear of losing his adherents, Polonius argued, "Has there ever been such a time – I would gladly know – that I have positively said 'This is so,' when it proved otherwise?"

"Not that I know," Claudius conceded.

Polonius pointed at his head, "Take *this*," he now indicated his neck, "from *this*, if this be otherwise: If circumstances lead me, I will *find* where the truth is hidden, though it were hidden indeed within the center of the Earth."

"How may we try it further?" Claudius wondered aloud more than asking Polonius.

Not that that stopped the Chamberlain from addressing the question. "You know ... sometimes he walks here in the lobby for several hours at a time ..."

Gertrude agreed, "So he does indeed."

"At such a time ... I'll loose my daughter to him." He turned once more to the King. "You and I will be behind the tapestry then, and mark the encounter – if he does *not* love her and does *not* fall from his reason on that account, let me no longer be assistant to this state beyond keeping a farm and carters."

Claudius nodded. "We will try it."

And even as her husband spoke, Gertrude happened to glance down an adjoining hallway ... and spied the distant figure of her disheveled son, studying a book and ambling their way. "But look, here comes the poor wretch, dejected and reading."

Polonius leaped into action. "Away, I do beseech you, both away – I'll accost him at once."

The King and Queen, and their ever-invisible attendants, hurried from the lobby scant moments before the unkempt Prince meandered into sight from the opposite direction.

Plastering upon his face what he considered his most disarming smile, Polonius called out, "Oh, give me leave: How are you, my good Lord Hamlet?" He strode boldly over to the reading man's side.

"Well," the Prince answered, "thank you."

Upon close inspection, Polonius saw that his daughter's word had been quite accurate – young Hamlet was in terrible shape. His clothes were in disarray, his hair was a mess, and ... well, he smelled bad.

"Do you ... know me, my lord?"

Hamlet's eyes drifted up from his clearly-captivating book for only the briefest moment. "Excellent well – you are a fishmonger."

Polonius blinked. "Not *I*, my lord."

"Then I *wish* you were so honest a man."

"*Honest*, my lord!" Polonius stammered, far more offended now than at any time during his trying conversation with the King.

"Aye, sir," Hamlet insisted. "To be honest, as this world goes, is to be one man picked out of ten thousand."

"That's ... very true, my lord."

"For if the sun breeds maggots in a dead dog, life from death, being flesh good enough for the sun to kiss— Have you a daughter?"

The Chamberlain could hardly keep up with the abrupt change of subject. "I ... have, my lord."

Closing his book for the first time (although he kept his place marked with his finger), the Prince drew Polonius closer, as though to impart some great secret. "Do not let *her* walk in the sun," he whispered urgently. "Conception is a blessing ... but not as your *daughter* may conceive." He smiled at Polonius' pale face and proclaimed in a regular voice, "Friend, look to it!" before continuing about his pacing circuit of the great lobby.

Polonius remained where he stood at first, staring after the deranged young man. *How say you by that? Still harping on my daughter. Yet did not even* know *me, not at first – he said I was a fishmonger! He is far gone, far gone ... and truly, in my youth, I suffered such extremes for love, very much like this. I'll speak to him again.* Hurrying the short distance that had grown between them, he asked,

"What do you read, my lord?"

"Words," the Prince answered. Confused, Polonius opened his mouth ... but wasn't certain what to say next. Had his question not been clear? Hamlet glanced over, saw the Chamberlain's bewilderment, and repeated, "*Words*." When that *still*, shockingly, did not answer the old man's question, he stated for the final time, "*Wooooooooooords*."

Dumbfounded, Polonius finally found his tongue. "What is the matter, my lord?"

"Between who?" Hamlet asked innocently.

"I mean, the *matter* – the *subject* – that you read, my lord."

Reacting as though he had just now been asked a meaningful question, Hamlet nodded and replied, "*Slanders*, sir: For the satirical rogue says here that old men ..." Though he never broke his stride, he ceased reading and began – strangely, it seemed, to the Chamberlain – to instead look Polonius up and down from head to toe as he continued, "... have grey beards, that their faces are wrinkled, their eyes discharging thick amber and plum-tree gum ... and that they have a plentiful lack of wit, together with most weak hams – all which, sir, though I most powerfully and potently believe, yet I find it *indecent* to have written it thus..."

Polonius' heart leaped into his throat as Hamlet suddenly slammed the book shut with an ear-piercing *crack*!

"For you yourself, sir," he continued, rounding on the man, "shall grow old as I am ... *if*, like a crab, you could go backward."

With that, Polonius could only stare with his jaw hanging low as, scuttling, the Prince of Denmark shuffled away from him like that very creature of the sea, away from the Chamberlain and toward the lobby's outdoors exit.

He's mocking me, the old man realized at long last. *This* may be *madness, but there is* reason *within it.* Yet still, if the young lord truly were mad, it was common knowledge that exposure to the unfettered elements might make such a condition worse ... wasn't it? He believed that he had read that somewhere ...

Gesturing beyond the Prince, he asked, "Will you walk out of the air, my lord?"

Snapping out of his burlesquing impression, Hamlet answered, quite seriously, "Into my grave."

"... indeed ... that *is* out of the air." For now, Polonius decided that he had had enough. *How witty his replies sometimes are! An appropriateness often struck by madness, from which reason and sanity could not so successfully be protected. I will leave him, and instead consider the arrangement of the meeting between him and my daughter.* "My honorable lord," he announced, this time allowing Hamlet to retreat from him, "I will most humbly take my leave of you."

"You cannot, sir, take from me *anything* that I will more willingly part with ..."

That insult was almost too much for Polonius. Here, here – he was the Lord Chamberlain of Denmark! And though young Hamlet was indeed heir to the throne, for now it was King *Claudius* whom he ultimately served!

And then, just as swiftly, his indignity was hampered when the Prince elaborated, "... except my life." He had said it, as well as his abusive dismissal, with an overly-zealous smile. But now, as though confused by his own words, he repeated with less relish, "... except my life ..." And, finally, with complete and utter gravity, "... except my life."

Silence hung before them for several heartbeats before Polonius, not knowing what else to say, hastened away with a weak, "Fare you well, my lord."

Hamlet stared after him ... and smirked. *These tedious old fools!*

As Polonius exited the room, he passed Rosencrantz and Guildenstern on their way in. "You go to seek the Lord Hamlet," he muttered in frustration, "there he is."

Guileless, Rosencrantz smiled. "Thank you, sir!"

Moving together toward the again-reading Prince, Guildenstern called aloud, "My honored lord!"

"My most dear lord!" Rosencrantz echoed.

Closing his book once more, Hamlet regarded his fellows students and smiled. "My excellent good friends! How are you ..." He thought for a moment. "Guildenstern? Ah, Rosencrantz! Good lads, how are you both?"

"As the common children of the earth," Rosencrantz answered with his customary simper.

"Happy, in that we are not *over-happy*," Guildenstern elaborated. "Alas, we have not yet reached the summit of fair Fortune's cap."

"Nor the soles of her shoe?"

Rosencrantz chuckled. "Neither, my lord."

"Then you live about her waist, or in the middle of her favors?"

Enjoying the linguistic joust, Guildenstern returned, "Faith, we are her ... privates." He winked.

Hamlet laughed openly at that. "In the secret parts of Fortune? Oh, most true – she *is* a strumpet. What's the news?"

"None, my lord, but that the world's grown honest."

"Then, dear Rosencrantz, Hell hath frozen over – but your news is not true." He grew a touch more serious. "Let me question more in particular: How have you, my good friends, so offended Fortune, that she sends you hither to this prison?"

That brought the pair up short. Guildenstern in particular was aghast. "*Prison*, my lord?!"

"Denmark is a prison."

Rosencrantz then decided that this must surely be another jest. He grinned and returned, "Then *the world* is one."

"A goodly one," the Prince agreed, "in which there are many confines, cells, and dungeons ... *Denmark* being one of the worst."

Now realizing that his friend was, indeed, quite serious, Rosencrantz argued, "*We* do not think so, my lord."

Hamlet shrugged. "Why, then, it is not so *to you* – for there is nothing either good *or* bad, but thinking makes it so: To *me*, it is a prison."

Guildenstern remained silent. Rosencrantz, on the other hand, believed he spied a way to turn this dark mood around. After all, wasn't that partly why the King had summoned them? "Why then, your *ambition* makes it a prison – 'tis too narrow for your great mind!"

"Oh, God," Hamlet muttered, turning and pacing away so that they had to follow to hear his next words. "I could be bounded in a nut shell and count myself a 'king of infinite space' ... were it not that I have such bad dreams."

Guildenstern joined in. "But dreams, indeed, *are*

ambition, for the very *goals* of the ambitious are merely the shadows of their dreams."

"A dream itself is but a shadow."

"Truly," Rosencrantz agreed heartily, "and *I* hold ambition in such airy and light regard that it is but a shadow's *shadow*."

"Then beggars, at least, possess their bodies, and our *monarchs* and strutting *heroes* are nothing but the beggars' shadows." Hamlet sighed, stroking his forehead as though suddenly afflicted with a headache. "Shall we go to the court? For, by my faith, I cannot argue."

"We'll attend you," they hurriedly assured him.

The Prince smirked. "I'll have no such thing. I will not associate you with the rest of my servants, for – to speak to you like an honest man – I am most *dreadfully* attended. But, in the well-worn way of friendship, what has brought you to Elsinore?"

"To visit *you*, my lord," Rosencrantz beamed, "no other occasion."

"Beggar that I am, I am even poor in *thanks* ... but I do thank you – and sure, dear friends, my thanks are not worth a halfpenny. Were you not sent for?" He looked one in the eyes, and then the other, taking full stock of them. Rosencrantz remained oblivious to the scrutiny, but Guildenstern withered somewhat. "Is it your *own* inclining? Is it a *voluntary* visitation? Come, deal honestly with me." When they did not speak, he raised his voice a touch. "Come, come. *Speak*."

Even Rosencrantz was feeling the tension now. Guildenstern shuffled and asked, "What should we say, my lord?"

Hamlet rolled his eyes. "Why, *anything*, it seems, except the truth: You *were* sent for; and there is a kind of confession in your expressions which your shame lacks the skill to hide." Whereas before he had been slowly raising his voice, his words now dropped to scarcely more than a whisper. "I *know* the good King and Queen have sent for you."

Fairly desperate to escape this pressure, Rosencrantz nearly begged, "To what *end*, my lord?"

"That, *you* must teach *me*. But let me compel you, by the rights of our fellowship, by the harmony of our youth, by the obligation of our ever-preserved *love* ... and by what more dear a more skillful exhorter could urge you with – be honest and direct with me, whether you were sent for ... or not?"

While Guildenstern had grown very, very still, as though he were afraid to move, Rosencrantz now squirmed and shuffled as though ants had invaded his undergarments. He turned to his comrade and panted, "What do you think?"

Hamlet eyed them closely. *Nay, then, I have an eye on you ... if you love me, do not hold back.*

At length, Guildenstern drew a slow breath, and confessed, "My lord ... we *were* sent for."

Both relieved by their honesty and frustrated at how difficult it had proven, Hamlet nodded. "*I* will tell you *why* – so shall my anticipation precede your disclosure, and your secrecy to the King and Queen not be the least impaired. I have recently – but *wherefore*, I know not – lost all my mirth, forgone all my usual exercises; and indeed, it goes so heavily with my disposition that this goodly frame – the Earth – seems to me a *sterile precipice*, this most excellent canopy

– the air – look you," he gestured grandly upward, toward some of the partially open apertures high above their heads, "this splendid, overhanging firmament, this majestical roof, adorned with golden fire ... why, it appears as nothing more to me than a foul and pestilent congregation of *vapors*."

The Prince shook his head and – much to his fellow students' confusion – suddenly seemed more taken with his own gesturing hand than the heavenly sky he had just been delineating. He wiggled his fingers, giggling like a child. "What a piece of work is a man! How *noble* in reason! How *infinite* in power! In form and moving, how exact and admirable! In action, how like an angel! In apprehension, how like a *god*!" He looked around, spinning wildly – Rosencrantz and Guildenstern each took a not-so-subtle step backward. "The beauty of the world! The paragon of animals!"

And then, just like that, Hamlet ceased his turning. He rocked to a halt before his audience, his expression again stern. "And yet, to me, what is this epitome of dust? Man delights not me ..." He focused his unyielding attention solely upon Rosencrantz, who had begun to smile. "... no, nor woman neither, though by your *smiling* you seem to say so."

Rosencrantz gulped. "My lord, there was no such stuff in my thoughts!"

"Why did you laugh then, when I said 'man delights not me'?"

Scrambling, Rosencrantz explained, "To think, my lord, if you 'delight not in man' ... what meager reception *the players* shall receive from you." To Rosencrantz's thick relief, Hamlet perked up upon this mention of the acting troupe. "We passed them on the way to Elsinore – and they, too, are coming here, to offer you *service*!"

And Hamlet was delighted indeed. "He that plays 'the King' shall be welcome – his 'majesty' shall have tribute from me; the adventurous knight shall use his sword and shield; the lover shall not sigh without due reward; the humorous man shall end his part in peace; the clown shall make those laugh whose lungs are easily tickled; and the lady shall say her mind freely and not omit the 'indecent' words, or the blank verse shall fall limp for it. What players are they?"

"Those very players you were wont to take delight in," Rosencrantz answered, "the tragedians of the city."

"But what circumstances have led to their traveling? Remaining in their home theatre served them better in both reputation and profit."

"I think their hindrance stems from the fascination with *younger* actors of late."

"Do they hold the same reputation they did when *I* was in London? Are they so followed?"

"No, indeed, they are not."

"How comes the 'War of the Theatres?' " the Prince asked, referring to the ongoing tension between old and new theatrical standards of recent years. "Do they grow rusty?"

"Nay, their endeavor keeps in the wonted pace. But there *is*, sir, a nest of children – little, immature hawks, the Children of the Chapel – that cry shrilly above others in controversy, and are most vehemently applauded for it. *These* are now the fashion, and they so satirize the 'common' theatres – so they call them – that many arm-bearing men of quality are *afraid* of their mighty pens, and scarcely dare to expose themselves to potential slander."

Hamlet scoffed. "What, are they *children*? Who maintains them? How are they supported? And this 'War of Theatres' – will *they* pursue the profession only until their voices change? Will they not continue afterwards, if they, too, should grow into mature players – as it is most likely, if their *means* are no better." He scowled. "Their writers do them wrong, to make them assail against their own future."

"In truth," Rosencrantz amended, "there has been much ado on *both* sides; and England sees nothing wrong in *inciting* them to controversy – there was, for a while, no money bid for the plot of a play, unless the poet and the player went to blows as part of the script."

Hamlet shook his head, the aspiring artist within him disgusted. "Is it possible?"

"Oh, there has been much throwing about of brains."

"Do they carry the day in victory?"

"Aye, that they do, my lord – Hercules and his load, too."

After a moment of thought, Hamlet merely sighed and shrugged. "It is not very strange; for my uncle is King of Denmark ... and those that would make mocking faces at him while my father lived, now give twenty, forty, fifty, even a hundred ducats a piece for a silver locket with a picture of him." He shook his head and muttered, "Christ's blood, there is something in this more than natural ... if philosophy could only find it out."

The moment hung heavy, and then Rosencrantz and Guildenstern gasped as a flourish of trumpets sounded throughout the castle lobby. The grand doors opened on cue, revealing the very acting troupe they had moments before been discussing.

"There are the players," Guildenstern pointed with relieved glee.

The Prince pivoted to them, his mood – gratefully, for them – again turning light and fair. "Gentlemen, you are welcome to Elsinore." He reached out with both arms. "Your hands, come then." They accommodated him, and he pulled them toward the approaching troupe, continuing, "The appropriate addition of welcome is fashion and ceremony: Let me observe the formalities with you in this manner, lest my courtesy to the players – which, I tell you, must show fairly outward – should appear more sincere than yours. You are welcome..." he lowered his voice, a slight smile worming its way across his lips, "... but my uncle-father and aunt-mother are *deceived*."

Guildenstern swallowed hard. "In what, my dear lord?"

"I am but mad north-north-west." He winked. "When the wind is *southerly* ... I know a hawk from a handsaw."

The bizarre reference – commentary on cutting tools? the weather? what possible connection could his lordship mean?! – left the students speechless and adrift. The Prince, for his part, seemed to delight in their predicament – *whatever* it meant, it clearly held meaning for *him* – and winked and chuckled at their discomfort.

Then from behind Hamlet came the Chamberlain's voice, "Well be with you, gentlemen!"

Hamlet's grin melted, but the mischievous gleam remained in his eye. He stepped around so that all three of them were facing the approaching Polonius, and he slipped an arm around each of their shoulders, pulling them forward into a huddle. When he spoke, it was in a stage-whisper, so that although it would be *difficult* for the old man to overhear, it would *not* be impossible. "Hark you, Guildenstern, and you, too – at each ear a hearer. That great baby you see there – in these parts, *some* call him 'Lord Chamberlain' – is not yet out of his newborn blankets."

"Perhaps he's come to them for the second time," Rosencrantz offered, struggling to return to the Prince's side of the joke, "for they say an old man enters a second childhood."

"I predict that he comes to tell me of the players, mark it." He then raised his voice considerably louder, as though following the thread of a non-existent conversation between the three, "You say right, sir – on Monday morning – it was indeed so."

"My lord," Polonius announced in his most official tone, "I have news to tell you."

"My lord, I have news to tell *you*," Hamlet returned. He then continued with "news" that had been *old* for hundreds of years. "When the legendary Roscius was an actor in Rome—"

Determined not to let the Prince get the better of his nerves again, Polonius pressed on with his business. "The actors have come hither, my lord."

"Buzz, buzz!" Hamlet snapped his fingers with impatience, rolling his eyes dramatically all the while.

Polonius bit back his first remark – a comment far too risky to unleash upon royalty, no matter what his position with the reigning King – and instead continued, "Upon my honor—"

" 'Then came each actor on his *ass* ...' "

Through gritted teeth, the Lord Chamberlain prevailed

... and unleashed a rehearsed onslaught that left Rosencrantz, Guildenstern, and even Hamlet staring upon him with open mouths. "The best actors in the world – either for tragedy, comedy, history, pastoral, pastoral-comical, historical-pastoral, tragical-historical, tragical-comical-historical-pastoral, scene undividable, or poem unlimited: Seneca's drama cannot be too heavy, nor Plautus' comedy too light ..." He paused for a breath, and realized that his listeners were looking upon him as though *he* – not the Prince – had taken leave of his senses. He resettled himself and, at last, summarized, "For strict observance of tradition, or freedom from it ... these are the *only* men."

"Oh Jephthah, judge of Israel," Hamlet marveled, and that roguish flitter still twinkled in his gaze, "what a treasure you had!"

Polonius blinked. "What a treasure he had, my lord?"

"Why, 'One fair daughter and no more, the which he loved passing well.' "

Still on my daughter, the Chamberlain marveled.

"Am I not in the right, old Jephthah?"

"If you call *me* Jephthah, my lord," Polonius nodded, "I have a daughter that I love passing well."

"Nay, *that* is not a given."

"What *is* a given, then, my lord?"

Hamlet practically danced around the old man – Guildenstern wondered what he and Rosencrantz had gotten themselves into. "Why, 'As by lot, God wot,' and then, you know, 'It came to pass, as most like it was,' – the first stanza of the pious song will show you more ... for look, where my interruption comes."

They followed his overly-grand gesture to see some four or five Players approaching them in humble fashion. Hamlet continued his little prance right over to them, proudly shaking hands and kissing cheeks. "You are *welcome*, masters – welcome, *all*. I am *glad* to see you well. Welcome, good friends. Oh, my old friend!" he seemed particularly pleased to see their leader, the mature and governing "First Player" amongst them. "Your face has curtained with a beard since I saw you last – have you come to confront and *beard* me in Denmark?" They laughed at the pun. "What, my young lady and mistress!" He scooped up the youngest – a little girl – into his arms. She giggled. "By our lady, your ladyship has grown nearer to Heaven than when I saw you last, by the altitude of a Venetian thick-soled shoe. Pray God, your voice – like a piece of raw gold – has not cracked into maturity so soon." He set the tittering girl back upon her feet and addressed them all. "Masters, you are all welcome. We'll even go to it like French falconers, fly at anything we see – we must have a speech straightaway!" He singled out the First Player once more. "Come, give us a taste of your skill – come, a *passionate* speech!"

"What speech, my lord?" the Player asked in a rich, commanding voice.

The Prince thought for a brief moment, then, "I heard you render a speech once, but it was never acted ... or, if it was, not more than once, for the play, I remember, did not please the mass audiences – it was too sophisticated for the common mind. But it *was* – as I received it, and others, whose judgments in such matters carried more authority than my own – an *excellent* play, the scenes well arranged, and set down with as much moderation as cunning. I remember, one said there were no spicy jokes in the lines to make the matter zesty, nor no matter in the phrase that might convict the author of pretense – but called it an *honest* method, as wholesome as sweet, and with more natural beauty than elaborate fashion. One speech in it I chiefly loved: It was Aeneas' tale to Dido, especially the portion where he speaks of the slaying of Priam at the fall of Troy. If it still lives in your memory, begin at this line: Let me see, let me see ..."

Hamlet thought hard again, then began briefly, " 'The rugged Pyrrhus, like the Hyrcanian beast—' " before waving at himself in frustration. "No, not like that ... ah, it begins with *Pyrrhus* ..."

And when he began again, it was with more confidence – and with no small talent for acting, Guildenstern quietly noted.

" 'The rugged Pyrrhus, he whose sable arms,
Black as his purpose, did the night resemble
When he lay couched in the ominous horse,
Hath now this dread and black complexion smear'd
With heraldry more dismal; head to foot
Now is he total gules; horridly trick'd
With blood of fathers, mothers, daughters, sons,
Baked and impasted with the parching streets,
That lend a tyrannous and damned light
To their lord's murder: Roasted in wrath and fire,
And thus o'er-sized with coagulate gore,

> With eyes like carbuncles, the hellish Pyrrhus
> Old grandsire Priam seeks ...' "

At long but still impressive length, Hamlet seemed to come up short of the speech that had clearly so moved him. Rather than let the tale fall short, he urgently waved for the Player to pick up where his failing had left off. "So, you proceed ..." he beseeched.

Clueless to the Prince's desire for lack of interruption, Polonius insisted on commenting, "Before God, my lord, well spoken, with good accent and good discretion." He might have continued, had Hamlet not impatiently waved him silent.

> Standing tall, the Player met the challenge before him ...
> " 'Anon he finds him
> Striking too short at Greeks; his antique
>   sword,
> Rebellious to his arm, lies where it falls,
> Repugnant to command: Unequal match'd,
> Pyrrhus at Priam drives; in rage strikes wide;
> But with the whiff and wind of his fell sword
> The unnerved father falls. Then senseless
>   Ilium,
> Seeming to feel this blow, with flaming top
> Stoops to his base, and with a hideous crash
> Takes prisoner Pyrrhus' ear: For, lo his sword,
> Which was declining on the milky head
> Of reverend Priam, seem'd I' the air to stick:
> So, as a painted tyrant, Pyrrhus stood,
> And like a neutral to his will and matter,
>   Did nothing.
> But, as we often see, against some storm,

A silence in the heavens, the rack stand still,
The bold winds speechless and the orb
    below
As hush as death, anon the dreadful thunder
Doth rend the region, so, after Pyrrhus'
    pause,
Aroused vengeance sets him new a-work;
And never did the Cyclops' hammers fall
On Mars' armour forged for proof eterne
With less remorse than Pyrrhus' bleeding
    sword
Now falls on Priam.
Out, out, thou strumpet, Fortune! All you
    gods,
In general synod 'take away her power;
Break all the spokes and fellies from her
    wheel,
And bowl the round nave down the hill of
    heaven,
As low as to the fiends ...!' "

Polonius grumbled, loudly and rudely, "This is too long."

"It shall be to the barbershop with your beard!" Hamlet snapped at the interruption. Polonius did not look quite as abashed as he'd hoped, but he turned back to the Player and urged him on. "Please, continue," he begged, dismissing the Lord Chamberlain, "he requires either a song-and-dance or a tale of bawdry, or else he sleeps. Say on – come to Hecuba."

The Player nodded and continued, " 'But who, O, who had seen the mobled queen—"

" 'The mobled queen?' " the Prince repeated, not certain that the Player had continued in the correct place.

Trying to please, Polonius offered, "That's good; 'mobled queen' is good."

" 'Run barefoot up and down,' " the Player pressed on, "'threatening the flames
With bisson rheum; a clout upon that head
Where late the diadem stood, and for a robe,
About her lank and all o'er-teemed loins,
A blanket, in the alarm of fear caught up;
Who this had seen, with tongue in venom
    steep'd,
'Gainst Fortune's state would treason have
    pronounced:
But if the gods themselves did see her then
When she saw Pyrrhus make malicious sport
In mincing with his sword her husband's
    limbs,
The instant burst of clamour that she made,
Unless things mortal move them not at all,
Would have made milch the burning eyes of
    heaven,
And passion in the gods.' "

Again, the Lord Polonius had apparently had enough. "Look," he said in what he felt was a compelling tone, "how he has grown pale and has tears in his eyes. Please, no more."

Hamlet sighed and forfeited. "It is well," he told the Player, "I'll have you recite the rest soon." He addressed Polonius, "My good lord, will you see the players well lodged? Do you hear, let them be *well treated* ... for they are the abstract and brief chronicles of the time – after your death, you would do better to have a bad epitaph than *their* ill report while you live."

"My lord, I will use them according to their merit."

Hamlet clapped his hands sharply. "Christ's blood, man, much better – use *every* man after his merit, and who should escape whipping? Use them after your own honor and dignity – the less *they* deserve, the more merit is in *your* bounty." He gestured to the broad doors. "Take them in."

"Come, sirs," Polonius called over his shoulder, leading them away.

"Follow him, friends." Hamlet grinned and announced, "We'll hear a play tomorrow!" As the rest of the players followed the old man, the Prince pulled the First Player aside. "Listen, old friend ... can you play *The Murder of Gonzago*?"

"Aye, my lord."

Hamlet clapped his hands once more. "We'll have it tomorrow night." He then paused, as though a thought had just occurred to him. "You could, if necessary, study a speech of some dozen or sixteen lines, which I would write and insert it in, could you not?"

The Player shrugged. "Aye, my lord."

"Very well. Follow that lord ... and see that you mock him *not*." He winked, and the Player chuckled, following the rest of his troupe. Hamlet then turned to his fellow students, "My good friends, I'll leave you until night: You are welcome to Elsinore."

"Good my lord!" Rosencrantz beamed with enthusiasm.

"Aye, so, God be with you."

He followed Rosencrantz and Guildenstern with his

eyes until they had withdrawn from his sight ...

... and then he sagged nearly to the floor, his hands resting on his knees, his head hanging low. His limbs trembled as though he had just run a marathon. And, indeed, he felt as though he had – a marathon of the *heart*.

Now I am alone ...

And then, with sudden ferocity, he slapped himself – *hard*.

Oh, what a rogue and base slave am I! Is it not monstrous that this player *here – but in a fiction, in a dream of passion – could force his soul so deep into his own imagination that, from its working, all his visage paled: Tears in his eyes, distraction in his demeanor, a broken voice, and his whole body fitting with expression to his mind? ... and all for* nothing!

"For Hecuba!" he burst aloud. He was so overwhelmed with self-loathing that he wanted to tear himself apart. He straightened and began to pace in a slow, laborious circle.

What's Hecuba *to him, or he to Hecuba, that he should weep for her? What would he do, had he the motive and the cue for passion that* I *have? He would* drown *the stage with tears and cleave the audience's ear with horrid speech, make* mad *the guilty and* appall *the innocent, astonish the ignorant, and amaze indeed the very faculties of eyes and ears ...*

"And yet ... *I*," he again spoke aloud, although this time he kept his voice to a whisper, lest someone witness his extended moment of scorn, "a dull-spirited rascal, mope about like a dreamy fellow, delaying my cause, and can say *nothing* – no, not for a *King*, upon whose crown and most dear life a damned destruction was made."

Am I a coward? he thought. *Who calls me villain? Breaks my pate across? Plucks off my beard, and blows it in my face? Tweaks me by the nose? Calls me the worst of all liars? Who does me this? Ha! By Christ's wounds, I should take it – for it cannot be but that I am meek and lack the gall to make me feel the bitterness of oppression ... or over this I should have made kites with this slave's entrails!*

"Bloody, bawdy villain!" he once more cursed audibly, and with his voice again heedlessly raised. How could he not? The world deserved to know of his shame! "Remorseless, treacherous, lecherous, unnatural *villain!* Oh, vengeance!" And then he stopped, looking about himself ... and laughed bitterly. "Why, what an *ass* I am! This is most brave, that *I* – the son of a dear father murdered, prompted to my revenge by Heaven and Hell – must, like a *whore*, unpack my heart with *words* ... and fall cursing, like a very drab, a kitchen menial serf!" He shook his head. "Fie upon it, damn it! Get to work, my brain!"

He paused, forcing himself to breathe slowly, concentrate ... concentrate ...

He had been on to something before ... when he had spoken to the Player. A nugget, a jewel that had occurred to him on the moment's notice ...

... when he asked the Player about inserting new material into the play.

I have heard that guilty creatures sitting at a play have been so struck *to the* soul *by the very cunning of the scene that at once, then and there, they have* proclaimed *their malefactions ... for murder, though it has no tongue, will speak with most miraculous power.* He allowed himself a small – oh, so small – smile of satisfaction. *I'll have these players enact something* like *the murder of my father before my uncle. I'll observe his expression, I'll probe him to the quick – if he but* flinches ... then *I know my course. After all, the spirit that I have seen* may *be the Devil ... and the Devil has the power to assume a pleasing shape. Yes, and perhaps out of my weakness and my melancholy, as he is very potent with such emotional states ... perhaps he* deludes *me to* damn *me.*

It was a thought that had crossed his mind more than once – a suggestion that Horatio had proposed the very night he had spoken to the ghost.

Yes, this way was better. This way, he could be *sure*.

I'll have grounds more relative than this. The play is the thing ... wherein I'll catch the conscience *of the* King.

PART THREE
CHAPTER ONE

The doors to the royal counsel chamber of Elsinore burst inward, and the reigning King erupted through them, followed closely by his wife. She, in turn, was followed not so closely by Polonius and his daughter, and then Rosencrantz and Guildenstern.

The King was not *quite* in "a rage" ... but, like an arthritic ache before a storm, all the signs were there. Upon inheriting the crown, he had adopted certain expectations – amongst them was the understanding that what the King wants, the King gets.

He was, therefore, disappointed with recent events ... to say the least.

"And can you, by *no* method of conversation," he demanded of the students, "get from him *why* he puts on this confusion, grating so harshly all his days of quiet with turbulent and dangerous *lunacy*?"

Guildenstern made to answer, but Rosencrantz spoke first. "He does confess he feels himself distracted ... but from what cause he will by no means speak."

Now Guildenstern offered quickly, "Nor do we find him willing to be probed, but, with a crafty 'madness,' he keeps aloof whenever we would bring him on to some confession of his true state."

"Did he receive you well?" the Queen asked.

"Most like a gentleman," Rosencrantz assured her.

"But with much constraint," Guildenstern amended.

Rosencrantz nodded his agreement. "He speaks sparingly ... but, of our questions, most generous in his reply."

"Did you tempt him?" the Queen asked. "To any pastime?"

Now Rosencrantz grinned, pleased to finally deliver what he perceived as good news. "Madam, it so happened that on the way here we passed certain players – of these actors we told him, and there did seem in him a kind of *joy* to hear of it. They are here in Elsinore, and, as I think, they have already arranged to play before him tonight."

"It's true," the Lord Chamberlain chimed in, "and he requested that I invite your majesties to hear and see the play as well."

Much to the assuagement of everyone in the room, the King smiled and released a deep, sincere sigh of relief. "With all my heart! And it greatly contents me to hear him so inclined." He spread his arms to the students. "Good gentlemen, give him a further encouragement, and *drive* his purpose on to these delights."

Rosencrantz answered proudly, "We shall, my lord." He and Guildenstern then turned about and left the counsel room.

A moment later, Claudius turned to his wife. "Sweet Gertrude, leave us, too – for we have privately sent for Hamlet to come here, so that he – as if it were by accident – may meet Ophelia here ..."

He gestured upward, and she followed his gaze. Should the need arise for the King of Denmark to host a larger counsel session than the usual – such as a gathering of all military leaders and their lieutenants – the spacious chamber was duly equipped with observation booths down the east and west sides of the room. Since these carrels were rarely used, their status quo left them closed off by heavy tapestries serving as drapes. Even before the King explained, the Queen believed that she understood – if one were poised within such a booth *without* removing the tapestry ...

Claudius continued, "Her father and myself – lawful observers – will so bestow ourselves that, seeing but unseen, we may judge their encounter frankly, and gather by his behavior, if it truly is the affliction of his love, or *not*, that he thus suffers for."

"I shall obey you." She turned to the young girl, taking her hands within her own. "And for your part, Ophelia, I do wish that your good beauties are the happy cause of Hamlet's madness – so shall I also hope that your *virtues* will bring him to his wonted way again, to both your honors."

Ophelia nodded earnestly. "Madam, I wish it may."

The Queen smiled and touched her cheek. It crossed her mind briefly to insist that she, too, join her husband and Chamberlain in observing the exchange ... but it pained her so to see her son's aberrant behavior, she could not trust herself to keep appropriately silent. Fighting tears, she made her exit.

Polonius took his daughter by the arm. "Ophelia, you walk here." He glanced over to Claudius. "If it so pleases your Grace, we will bestow ourselves." The King nodded once, sharply, and moved to the narrow steps which led to their chosen alcove. But before following his liege, Polonius again turned to Ophelia and withdrew something from within his voluminous robes. "Read on this doctrinal book – that show of such a religious practice may help make your solitude seem ... natural." He sighed. "We are often to blame in this – it is too often proved true – that with devotion's visage and pious demeanor, we do sugar over the Devil himself."

Claudius, who had halted at the foot of the steps to await the Chamberlain, closed his eyes briefly as he contemplated the old man's words – words directed at his daughter, but which found their way deeply into the King's own heart.

Oh, it is too true! How painful a lashing that sentiment gives my conscience! The harlot's cheek, beautied with plastering makeup, is not more ugly compared to the cosmetics that cover it than is my deed compared to my most painted word. Oh, heavy burden!

"I hear him coming," Polonius announced, snapping all three of them to attention. He hurried to join his King. "Let us withdraw, my lord." In a rush, the two men climbed the steps, and concealed themselves.

A door at the far end opened, revealing the somber Hamlet. He took only a cursory glance around the room and – seeing neither the expected King, nor the unexpected Ophelia as yet – he returned his focus to the object in his hand. Slowly, he entered, the object monopolizing his attention.

From their seclusion, Polonius could not make out the item in question, but Claudius recognized it – it was a locket, most likely one of royal design. Claudius' own regime had made his image in a casing of silver, but Hamlet's appeared to be one of gold, offering Claudius a solid guess as to whose likeness the Prince viewed.

And he was correct. The image within was not that of

Claudius, but of King Hamlet. The late King's son gazed upon it with such deep depression that he felt as though the air around him had grown unbearably thick and cold. Hamlet tried to convince himself that he merely had to wait until that very evening, upon which his doctored play should answer the question of Claudius' guilt once and for all. But still, to wait so long, so long ... and his heart had felt so heavy even *before* the ghost had appeared ...

With a pained sigh, he slipped the locket back into the confines of his doublet. Shuffling forward, his voice leaked from him in a whisper that frustrated those who spied upon him.

"To be, or not to be: That is the question," he breathed to himself, to the universe, to no one. "Whether it is nobler in the mind to submit to the slings and arrows of whimsical fortune ... or to *battle* against a sea of troubles, and by opposing them, *end* them. To die ... to *sleep*, nothing more ... and by 'a sleep' to say we end the heartache and the thousand natural shocks that flesh is heir to ... oh, it is a *conclusion* to be devoutly wished." He closed his eyes for a moment, yearning for such a painless void ... until his mind took the next, inevitable step – for when is man ever truly content to accept a gift without question? "To die, to sleep ... but to sleep is perchance to *dream* – aye, *there's* the dilemma. For in that sleep of death, when we have freed ourselves from the turmoil of this mortal life ... we must pause and contemplate what dreams may come! *There's* the consideration that makes the afflicted person live so long, for who would knowingly bear the whips and scorns of the world – the oppressor's wrong, the proud man's insolence, the pangs of despised love, the law's delay, the insolence of politicians, and the insults that patient merit of the unworthy takes – when he might *release himself* from this life with a mere dagger? Who would bear burdens, to grunt and sweat under a weary life ... but that the dread of something *after* death – that undiscovered country from whose borders no traveler returns – paralyzes the will and makes us prefer to bear those ills we have than to fly to others of which we do not know? Thus, *conscience* makes *cowards* of us all! And thus, the healthy complexion of resolution is sicklied over with the pale tinge of brooding ... and with this regard, enterprises of great dignity and importance turn their currents awry ... and lose the name of *action* ..."

By now, Hamlet's dark languishing had brought him much closer to the trap laid for him. Ophelia, her heart in her throat and its beat pounding through her head, focused all of her attention upon Polonius' book just as the Prince finally noticed her.

When his mind finally absorbed exactly *who* he was seeing, Hamlet stopped short. *Quiet you, now!* he scolded himself for having spoken such thoughts aloud, even in seeming private. *It is the fair Ophelia!*

And oh, how he had missed her. Since the death of his father, and even more since the appearance of the ghost claiming to be the spirit of his father, to say that Hamlet had been "preoccupied" would be an understatement for the annals of time. But still ... the Prince did recall a happier time, when his father sat alive and robust upon the throne, his mother was not yet a cheating, incestuous whore, and his affections yearned for *this* fair beauty, rather than death.

Slowly, tentatively, he approached her. Ophelia, for her part, affected a reasonable amount of surprise upon "first" seeing him as he drew near. He smiled, glanced down at the book in her hands, then around at the apparently empty room, and finally back to her. "Nymph, in thy prayers," he said, "be all my sins remembered."

"Good afternoon, my lord," she returned his smile. "How have you faired all this long time?"

Aye, he agreed inwardly. *So long a time. Too long.* "I humbly thank you—"

He heard it then. Perhaps not so much "heard" as *felt* it. A creak, a rustle, a breath ... *something.* Above and behind him. As casually as he could, he glanced over his shoulder, and caught just the slightest, minuscule shift of the tapestry ... the tapestry behind which spied, most likely, the very poser-King and dawdling, old fool who had summoned him to this place.

"Well, well, well," he whispered under his breath. *So ...* that's *it, is it?*

Hamlet shifted his whole focus back to Ophelia. His lovely Ophelia ... his sweet Ophelia ...

... his *traitorous* Ophelia!

Oh, he knew that her father and his uncle-father were certainly behind this little deception. Ophelia would be, at best, a nervous pawn at their disposal. But he had more than enough betrayal filling his stomach this day – he would imbibe no more!

They wanted a telling display, did they? Well, then ... he would *give* them one!

In the meantime, Ophelia – unaware that the game was up – continued speaking to him. "My lord, I have remembrances of yours, that I have long wished to redeliver to you." She pulled from her pocket a necklace, a pendant, and a small, crudely-whittled, wooden rose. "I pray you," she said, sadly, "now receive them."

"No, not I," he retorted sharply, just loud enough so that *all* ears would hear his words. "I never gave you anything."

Ophelia blinked in confusion, and hurt. As guilty as she had felt participating in this charade, she now felt a degree of her own anger at this blatant lie. "My honored lord," she chastised him, "you know right well you did! And, with them, words composed of such sweet breath that they made the things more rich. Now, their perfume is lost, and I ask you to take these back; for to the noble mind, rich gifts wax *poor* when givers prove unkind." She attempted to press the three objects into his hands. "There, my lord."

But Hamlet shoved the baubles aside. "Ha, ha! Are you chaste?"

Again, Ophelia was bewildered. "My lord?"

"Are you beautiful?" He slowly began to circle her.

"What ... does your lordship mean?"

"That if you are both chaste and beautiful, your chastity should allow *no one* to converse with your beauty."

Ophelia's cheeks reddened. "Could beauty, my lord, have *better* intercourse than with chastity?" she returned with heat.

Hamlet laughed sardonically at her attempt to turn his words against him, to keep up with, and even top, his insult to her sexuality. "Aye, truly; for the power of beauty will sooner transform chastity into a *harlot* than the force of chastity can translate beauty into its own likeness." He thought of his mother and mused, "This was once a paradox, but now time has given it *proof*." Then he scoffed, eyeing Ophelia with something almost akin to hate. "I did love you once."

"Indeed, my lord, you made me believe so."

The Prince rounded on her, prompting her to take a nervous step away from him. "You should *not* have believed me! For virtue cannot so alter our sinful nature, that we cannot still taste of it." He spat the next words venomously. "I - loved - you - *not.*"

Tears formed in Ophelia's eyes. "I was the more deceived."

Disgusted, Hamlet started to march away from her. And why not? Perhaps he should advance upon the spying King, throttle him here and now, and be done with it! But then he reined himself in – a bit – and so turned once again upon the girl, placing his face inches from hers until she retreated even further from him.

"Get thee to a *nunnery,*" he commanded. "Why would you be a breeder of *sinners*? I am myself tolerably virtuous ... but yet, I could accuse myself of such things that it would be better if my mother had not borne me! I am very proud, revengeful, ambitious, with more offences at my command than I have thoughts to put them in, imagination to give them shape, or time to act them in. What should such fellows as I do, crawling between Earth and Heaven? We are arrant knaves, all – believe *none* of us. Go thy ways to a nunnery."

Then, abruptly, deliberately, he calmed and stood straight. As though just now recalling his reasons for being here, he looked around. This would be her one chance – her *only chance* – to at least partially redeem herself in his eyes.

"Where's your father?" he asked in a low voice – low enough that, if she responded in kind, she could answer truthfully without her taskmasters hearing.

For a moment, he thought she might confess. If she did, if only she did! Then he might, just might, be able to ...

But then she answered, "... at home, my lord."

Rage surged through Hamlet with such ferocity, he could barely keep from striking her, or throttling her ... or both. He released what must have sounded like a barbarous bark to those bearing witness, and raised his voice for all to hear.

"Let the doors be shut upon him," he announced, "that he may play the fool nowhere but in his *own* house!" He snarled at Ophelia one last time, then made to leave. "Farewell."

She eyed him like the madman he nearly was. "Oh, help him, you sweet Heaven!" she pleaded under her breath ...

... but not so low that the Prince did not catch her prayer. He whirled upon her once again, and this time he seized her arm – hard enough to bruise, she would later discover – so that she could not pull away from him.

"If you *do* marry," he growled, "I'll give you *this* plague for your dowry: Be you as chaste as ice, as pure as snow, you shall not escape defamation. Get you to a nunnery, go, farewell!" He pointed with his free hand, but did not release her. He then continued on, as though she had *chosen* not to take her exit. "Or, if you feel the need to marry, marry a *fool*; for *wise* men know well enough what monsters you women make of them. To a nunnery, go, and quickly, too. Farewell!"

Again he pointed, but again he did not release her. Terrified, her breath rasped through her throat. "Oh Heavenly powers, restore him!" she prayed aloud.

She yelped as he suddenly pinched her cheek. He then

turned his makeup-smeared fingers around for both of their scrutiny. "I have heard of your paintings, too, well enough!" He wiped the cosmetics upon the front of her bodice. As he ranted, he did the same with her lipstick – pinching her bottom lip, examining the red smear, and then staining her bodice with it. "God has given you one face, and you make yourselves another! You jig, you amble, and you lisp, and nick-name God's creatures, and affected ignorance to cover your wantonness! Go to, I'll have no more of it! It has *made me mad*!"

With that, he shoved her away so harshly that she fell to the floor. Until now, she'd managed to hold on to his former gifts, as well as her father's book of prayers. No more. They scattered in all directions as, crying, she scrambled away from the Prince on her hands and knees.

Hamlet spun in a circle, bellowing his words so that they echoed from the walls. "I say, we will have *no more marriages*!" He then slowed his turn, until he stood still, looking upward, facing one very specific tapestry. "Those that are married already ... all *but one* shall live ... the rest shall remain as they are."

He stood like that for a moment, staring daggers at the hidden alcove and the not-so-secret audience within. Then, almost as an afterthought, he glanced over at the horrified Ophelia. "To a nunnery, go," he commanded one final time...

... and then turned on his heel and left.

Still crying, Ophelia stared after him. *Oh, what a noble mind is here overthrown! The courtier's eye, soldier's sword, scholar's tongue; the hope and pride of a kingdom made fair by his very presence, the very idea of fashion and the utmost model of proper behavior, the observed of all observers ... fallen quite, quite down! And I – of ladies most deject and wretched – that sucked the honey of his musical vows, now see that noble and most sovereign reason, like sweet bells jangled, are out of tune and harsh; that unmatched form and feature of full blown youth, now withered with madness ... oh, woe is me, to have seen what I have seen, see what I see!*

She buried her face in her hands, and sobbed.

Slowly, the King and Lord Chamberlain emerged from their stairwell. Polonius' robes were in a bit of disarray, as Claudius had been forced – more than once – to prevent the older man from rushing to his daughter's rescue. Even now, Polonius fell upon his little girl, pulling her to him and offering what comfort his arms could provide.

King Claudius stood alone, staring down at the whittled rose, a once-gift from his nephew and son. In the scuffle, it had broken in two.

"Love!" he mused bitterly. "His affections do not tend that way; nor what he said, though it lacked a little in form ... was *not* like 'madness.' There's something in his soul, over which his melancholy sits on brood; and I do fear the hatch and the disclosure will be some *danger* ..." He looked to the Lord Chamberlain, and found that Polonius was already meeting his gaze. "... for which to prevent, I have in quick determination thus set it down: He shall go with speed to *England*, for the demand of our neglected tribute. Hopefully, the seas and countries, different with a variety of sights, shall expel this ... something-settled matter in his heart, whereon his *brain's* constantly hammering puts him this far from his normal behavior. What do you think of that?"

Polonius waffled. "It shall do well ... but ... I *still* believe that the origin and commencement of his troubles sprung from neglected love." Ophelia started to speak, and he hushed her with a gentle, loving stroke of her hair. "How now, Ophelia! You need not tell us what Lord Hamlet said; we heard it *all*." He regarded the King once more. "My lord, do as you please, but ... if you hold it fit, after the play tonight, allow his Queen mother, alone, to entreat him to *share* his troubles. Let her be blunt with him ... and *I* will be placed, so please you, within earshot of their conference. If she does not learn the truth from him, then send him to England ... or confine him where your wisdom thinks best."

Claudius nodded. "It shall be so ... for madness, in great ones, must *not* unwatched go."

PART THREE
CHAPTER TWO

"Speak the speech, I pray you," Hamlet instructed one of the players as they marched through a castle hallway, "rapidly and neatly on the tongue, as I pronounced it to you. But if you exaggerate your diction, as many of your players do, I might have allowed the town-crier to speak my lines."

The player chuckled, and shook his head reassuringly.

Hamlet continued, "Nor do not saw the air too much with your hand, like this," he gestured about, over-dramatically, "but use all motions gently; for in the very torrent, tempest, and, as I may say, the whirlwind of passion, you must achieve and inspire a moderation that may give it *smoothness*. Oh, it offends me to the soul to hear a boisterous, wigged fellow tear a passion to tatters, to very *rags*, to split the ears of even the low-cast groundlings, who for the most part are able to take in nothing but inexplicable dumbshows and noise – I would have such a fellow whipped for overdoing the Saracen god, Termagant; as it out-does even the declamatory Herod himself ... please, avoid it."

The player nodded deeply and promised, "I warrant your honor."

But the Prince was not yet at ease. He continued his instruction, "Do not be too *tame* neither, but let your own discretion be your tutor – suit the action to the word, and the word to the action; with this special overstep, not the moderation of nature, for anything so overdone is contrary to the purpose of *acting*, whose end – both at the first and now – was and is to hold, as it were, the mirror up to nature; to show *virtue* her own features, *scorn* her own image, and the very age and body of *time* his form and impression. Now, if this is overdone, or comes off inadequately, though it may make the *undiscriminating* laugh, it cannot help but make the knowledgeable *grieve*; the judgment of even *one* of whom must, in your estimation, outweigh a whole theatre of the others." He made a distasteful face as he confessed, "Oh, there are players that I have seen play, and heard *others* praise, and highly ... not to speak irreverently, but they have neither the accent of the decent nor the gait of Christian, pagan, or *any* man whatsoever, and have so strutted and bellowed that I have thought perhaps some of Nature's *apprentices* had made such men, and *not* made them well, for they imitated humanity so *abominably*."

At length, the player felt the need to address the Prince's rather sensitive concerns. "I hope," he interjected humbly, "that we have reformed that fairly *well* with us, sir."

"Oh, reform it *altogether*," Hamlet insisted. "And let those that play your clowns speak no more than is set down for them! For there are *some* that will laugh at themselves, as though to set on some quantity of witless spectators to laugh along, too ... and, in the meantime, some necessary portion of the play fails to be considered. Such behavior is *villainous*, and shows a most pitiful ambition in the fool that uses it."

As he said this last bit, the Prince and the player reached the end of the hallway. He glimpsed the approaching forms of Rosencrantz, Guildenstern, and the Lord Chamberlain, and decided it was time to let the player off the hook.

"Go," he commanded the actor with a smile and a clap

on the shoulder, "make yourself ready." The player bowed and slipped away, just as the newcomers drew within earshot. "How now, my lord! I hope the King will hear this masterpiece?"

The old man beamed. "And the *Queen*, too, and that presently."

Hamlet grinned and snapped his fingers, gesturing Polonius away. "Bid the players make haste."

Polonius, clearly displeased with such an abrupt dismissal, nevertheless nodded and followed after the receding player.

Hamlet then turned, folded his arms, and regarded the students with an air of impatience. "Will you two help to hasten them?" he asked, though it was clear that he was not "asking" at all.

Guildenstern glanced anxiously at Rosencrantz before they said together, "We will, my lord," and beat their own retreat.

The Prince sighed and turned away before glimpsing the approach of a much more *welcome* figure. "What ho! Horatio!"

"Here, sweet lord," his friend announced before taking his hand, "at your service."

"Horatio, you come as close to being a righteous man as anyone with whom I have ever conversed."

Horatio blushed deeply. "Oh, my dear lord—"

"Nay, do not think I *flatter*; for what advancement may I hope from you who has no revenue but your good spirits to feed and clothe you? Why should the poor be flattered? No, let the flattering tongue lick tasteless pomp, and crook the easily bent hinges of the knee where profit may follow fawning." He waggled his finger. "Do you hear? Since my dear soul was mistress of Fortune's choice and could distinguish men, her choice has sealed you for herself; for you have been such a man – in suffering all, that suffers nothing – that Fortune's buffets and rewards has taken with equal thanks ... and blessed are those whose passions and judgment are so well blended, that they are not a pipe for Fortune's finger to play whatever note she please. *Give me* that man that is not passion's slave, and I will wear him in my heart's core – aye, in my heart of hearts – as *I* do *you* ..."

At last, the Prince seemed to realize that he'd launched into this diatribe with no warning for his friendly victim ... who, of course, would never voice a complaint.

"Something too much of this," he dismissed himself, waving the topic away. He then placed his hand on Horatio's shoulder and drew him closer. "There is a play tonight, shown before the King – one *particular* scene of it comes very near the circumstances which I have told you of my father's death. I ask of you, when you see that act performed, with the most intense observation of your soul: *Observe ... my ... uncle!* If his hidden guilt does not unleash itself in one speech ... then it *is* an evil spirit that we have seen, and my imaginations are as foul as the armorer god Vulcan's forge. Pay *close* attention to him, for I, too, will rivet my eyes to his face, and afterward we will join both our judgments and reach a verdict on his behavior."

Horatio nodded his understanding. "It is well, my lord. If he steals anything while this play is playing, and escapes detection, *I* will pay for the theft."

Hamlet smiled, and squeezed his friend's shoulder warmly. Then he heard an approaching commotion, and knew that time grew short. "They are coming to the play – and *I* must continue the pretense of madness. Get to your place."

He turned Horatio, and together they passed through the short entryway into the stadium theater of Elsinore.

They were just in time. A flourish of trumpets sounded a traditional Danish march, followed closely by a corps of kettle-drums. The sizable audience stood as one as the King and Queen entered, her hand resting upon his raised forearm.

Close behind them were Polonius and his daughter, the ever-sweet Ophelia, as well as Hamlet's student friends – apparently, it had taken them no time at all to square away the players, and to find their way back into the royal graces.

Hamlet ground his teeth and forced a giddy smile, even as Horatio fell away into the background.

"How fares our cousin Hamlet?" the King asked, with his voice raised in typical show.

"Excellent, in faith," Hamlet returned with equal volume, "of the chameleon's dish: I eat the air, promise-crammed – you cannot feed capons so."

Claudius blinked, his eyes flickered oh-so-briefly to his wife in confusion. "I can make nothing of this answer, Hamlet; these words are not mine."

"No, nor mine now." Hamlet turned to the Lord Chamberlain, "My lord, you played once in the university, you say?"

Polonius glowed. "That did I, my lord, and was accounted as a good actor."

"What did you enact?"

He thought back for a moment, though Hamlet suspected this was more in show than a true search of memory. "I did enact *Julius Caesar*: I was killed in the Capitol – Brutus killed me."

Hamlet shook in head in mock shame. "It was a brute action of him to kill so *capital* a calf there." Only Rosencrantz chuckled under his breath, which drew the Prince's attention around to him. "Are the players ready?"

"Aye, my lord; they wait for your leisure."

"Come hither, my dear Hamlet," the Queen called as she moved to her place by the King's throne. She gestured to the seat on her other side. "Sit by me."

"No, good mother," Hamlet declined, "here's metal more attractive." With a spin, he danced over before the startled Ophelia – who had quietly found her own place – and stretched himself full-length upon the bench beside her.

Polonius immediately nudged the King and whispered, "Oh, ho! Do you see that?"

Hamlet proceeded to inch his way even closer to Ophelia, deliberately invading her space. "Lady, shall I lie in your lap?"

"*No*, my lord," she answered flatly.

"I mean," the Prince clarified, the picture of innocence, "my *head* upon your *lap*?"

Swallowing a sigh, Ophelia granted, "Aye, my lord," and moved her arm to oblige him.

Hamlet smirked, making himself thoroughly comfortable. "Do you think I meant something *indecent*?"

"I think nothing, my lord," she said, eyes forward.

"*That's* a fair thought to lie between maids' legs."

"What is, my lord?"

" 'Nothing'."

"You are merry, my lord," she observed dryly.

"Who, *I*?"

"Aye, my lord."

He shrugged, adjusting his head upon her thigh. "Oh God, I am your very best farcical jig-maker. What should a man do but be merry?" He gestured absently beyond her, glancing at the Queen from his upside-down perspective. "For, look you, how cheerfully my mother looks, and my father died within these two hours."

Treading carefully, Ophelia licked her lips and corrected, "Nay, it is almost four *months* now, my lord."

Hamlet appeared surprised, though there was a wily glint in his eye. "So long? Nay then, to the Devil with my black garments, for I'm ready to don a suit of fine fur!" He raised his voice, to ensure that their many eavesdroppers were well catered. "Oh, heavens! Died four months ago, and not forgotten yet? Then there's hope a great man's memory may outlive his life *half a year* – but, by your lady, he must build churches, then; or else he shall suffer being forgotten, with the hobby-horse, whose epitaph is 'For, O, for, O, the hobby-horse is forgot.' "

To say that the vicinity had fallen into an "uncomfortable silence" would have been an understatement, and there were many sighs of relief – some inward, but a few notably outward – as the high-pitched hautboys sounded and the dumb-show began.

Upon the stage a player-king and -queen entered, each embracing the other with a loving gaze in their over-powdered faces. The queen knelt before her liege, making grand gestures of proclamation unto him. He pulled her close and rested his head upon her neck. Slowly, they made their mutual way to the ground, him lying upon a bank of flowers.

Once the queen saw that he was asleep, she kissed her finger tips, brushed them against his cheek, then slipped away, off stage-left.

Almost immediately, a black-clad figure slipped in from stage-right. He crept near the sleeping king, pulled the crown from the king's head, and then deftly produced a vial from his sleeve. Uncapping the small flagon, he poured its contents into the king's ear, then dashed away as swiftly as he had arrived.

Momentarily, the player-queen returned, found her player-king dead, and began making cumbersome signs of sorrow.

The black-clad poisoner, accompanied by three mutes, returned in a less-furtive demeanor. He joined her beside her dead husband's body, and for a time he seemed to mourn with her, even as the mutes carried the body away.

Soon, however, the poisoner's performance shifted from sadness to flirtation. He produced a gift – a silver locket – and offered it to her.

She turned away, disgust upon her face.

He moved around, producing a second gift – a rose – and extended one in each hand.

She resisted again, but with less vehemence.

Finally, her courter moved in with locket, rose ... and a kiss upon her cheek. She smiled, draped her hand upon his forearm, and they exited the stage, together.

Confused by it all, Ophelia whispered, "What does this mean, my lord?"

"Why, this is skulking mischief," he replied innocently, his eyes shifted toward the granite-still King of Denmark.

"Does this show summarize the plot of the play?"

On the stage, the Prologue entered.

"We shall know by this fellow," Hamlet indicated. "The players cannot keep secrets; they'll tell all."

"Will he tell us what this dumb-show meant?"

"Aye, or *any* show that you'll show him – if you are not ashamed to show, he'll not be ashamed to tell you what it means."

Ophelia rolled her eyes, as much as she dared toward the Prince of her nation. "You are naughty, you are *wicked*. I'll watch the play."

Below, the Prologue announced in a robust voice:

"For us, and for our tragedy,
here bowing to your clemency,
we beg your hearing patiently."

He then spun on his heel and marched off-stage.

Now it was Hamlet's turn to roll his eyes. He mused in a fairly loud voice, "Is this a *prologue*, or the short inscription on a *ring*?"

"It *is* brief, my lord," Ophelia agreed.

"As woman's love," he retorted, again making sure that his voice carried well enough to be heard by the King and Queen. His mother smarted visibly, but still Claudius remained stoic.

Now two players came back into view – they were dressed differently, but it was obviously the same player-king and -queen as before, and equally evident that they bore the same roles. He sat upon an oversized, wooden throne, and she draped herself at his side.

The king spoke first ...

"Full thirty times hath Phoebus' cart gone

round
Neptune's salt wash and Tellus' orbed ground,
And thirty dozen moons with borrow'd sheen
About the world have times twelve thirties
    been,
Since love our hearts and Hymen did our
    hands
Unite commutual in most sacred bands."
The queen replied ...
"So many journeys may the sun and moon
Make us again count o'er ere love be done!
But, woe is me, you are so sick of late,
So far from cheer and from your former state,
That I distrust you. Yet, though I distrust,
Discomfort you, my lord, it nothing must:
For women's fear and love holds quantity;
In neither aught, or in extremity.
Now, what my love is, proof hath made you
    know;
And as my love is sized, my fear is so:
Where love is great, the littlest doubts are
    fear;
Where little fears grow great, great love
    grows there."
The king ...
" 'Faith, I must leave thee, love, and shortly
    too;
My operant powers their functions leave to
    do:
And thou shalt live in this fair world behind,
Honour'd, beloved; and haply one as kind
For husband shalt thou –"

Queen ...

"O, confound the rest!

Such love must needs be treason in my
    breast:

In second husband let me be accurst!

None wed the second but who kill'd the first."

Through all of this, Hamlet divided his attention
between a show of watching the players, and secretly eyeing
both his mother and uncle as closely as he could. Gertrude's
discomfort was now evident for all to see, and even the stolid
Claudius had begun to shift a little. Neither of them looked
his way.

"That's wormwood," he muttered under his breath,
"harsh wormwood ..."

Queen:

"The instances that second marriage move

Are base respects of thrift, but none of love:

A second time I kill my husband dead,

When second husband kisses me in bed."

King:

"I do believe you think what now you speak;

But what we do determine oft we break.

Purpose is but the slave to memory,

Of violent birth, but poor validity;

Which now, like fruit unripe, sticks on the
    tree;

But fall, unshaken, when they mellow be.

Most necessary 'tis that we forget

To pay ourselves what to ourselves is debt:

What to ourselves in passion we propose,

The passion ending, doth the purpose lose.

The violence of either grief or joy

Their own enactures with themselves
destroy:

Where joy most revels, grief doth most
lament;

Grief joys, joy grieves, on slender accident.

This world is not for aye, nor 'tis not strange

That even our loves should with our fortunes
change;

For 'tis a question left us yet to prove,

Whether love lead fortune, or else fortune
love.

The great man down, you mark his favorite
flies;

The poor advanced makes friends of
enemies.

And hitherto doth love on fortune tend;

For who not needs shall never lack a friend,

And who in want a hollow friend doth try,

Directly seasons him his enemy.

But, orderly to end where I begun,

Our wills and fates do so contrary run

That our devices still are overthrown;

Our thoughts are ours, their ends none of our
own:

So think thou wilt no second husband wed;

But die thy thoughts when thy first lord is
dead."

Queen:

"Nor earth to me give food, nor heaven light!

Sport and repose lock from me day and
night!

To desperation turn my trust and hope!
An anchor's cheer in prison be my scope!
Each opposite that blanks the face of joy
Meet what I would have well and it destroy!
Both here and hence pursue me lasting
    strife,
If, once a widow, ever I be wife!"

At this proclamation, Hamlet barked a short, harsh round of laughter, the sarcasm nearly dripping upon those closest to him. "If she should break it now!" he chided.

Again, neither Gertrude nor Claudius so much as glanced at him – their lack of reaction, in light of his jarring interruption was far more telling than any sullied look they might have given him ... which Ophelia was more than happy to provide.

The player-king now worked his way from the mock-throne, eventually lying upon the same bed of flowers as before. As he moved, he spoke ...

"'Tis deeply sworn. Sweet, leave me here
    awhile;
My spirits grow dull, and fain I would beguile
The tedious day with sleep."

As he drifted away, the queen stroked his cheek once more ...

"Sleep rock thy brain,
And never come mischance between us twain!"

With that, she repeated the kissing-fingertips gesture, and exited to the familiar stage-left.

Hamlet rocked forward, lifted his left leg, and spun on his buttocks so that he now straddled the bench beneath him. He looked past the startled Ophelia and asked his mother, directly and loudly, "Madam, how do you like this play?"

Caught off-guard, hopelessly rattled and unprepared, Gertrude managed to force a weak chuckle and reply, "The lady *protests* too much, I think ..."

"Oh, but she'll *keep* her word," Hamlet commented with innocent vehemence.

At last, Claudius spoke – though he still would not look Hamlet in the eye. "Have you heard the argument? Is there no offense in it?"

Hamlet was well aware that the King meant "offensive subject matter," but he chose to take his words quite literally. Almost batting his eyelashes, he answered, "No, no, they do but *jest*, poison in *jest* – no offense in the world!"

Claudius grumbled something under his breath, then spoke up. "What do you call the play?"

" 'The Mouse-Trap.' Marry, how? *Figuratively*. This play is the representation of a murder done in Vienna: *Gonzago* is the duke's name; his wife, *Baptista*, you shall see again shortly." Hamlet shook his head in over-the-top admiration for the players below. "It *is* a villainous piece of work ... but what of that? Your majesty and we that have free, *guiltless* souls ... why, it cannot touch *us*!" He smiled giddily, slapping his knee. "Let only the chafed horse wince – *our* backs are untouched!"

He then noticed that a new player had emerged on stage. "This is one Lucianus, nephew to the king," he explained.

"You are as good at summarizing the action as a chorus," Ophelia commented, "my lord."

"I could recite the dialogue between you and your love," Hamlet replied, "as though I were a puppet-master."

Ophelia sniffed and looked away once more, her eyes

locked fiercely upon the player-Lucianus. "You are bitter, my lord, you are *sharply* bitter."

"It would cost you a groaning to take off my sharp edge."

Ophelia blushed and shook her head. "Sharper still, and *more* bitter."

Hamlet shrugged. "And so, for better or worse, you mislead your husbands." He then called out to the posturing but still-silent player below. "*Begin*, murderer! A pox upon you, *forget* your damnable facial expressions, and *begin*!" He clapped his hands loudly, harshly, causing Ophelia and others around him to jump. "Come: 'The croaking raven doth bellow for revenge!' "

The player-Lucianus stuttered for a heartbeat, then his training took over, and he spoke as though he had not been interrupted:

"Thoughts black, hands apt, drugs fit, and
time agreeing;
Confederate season, else no creature
seeing;"

Just as in the dumb-show, a small flagon appeared from within his sleeve. He clutched the little bottle between thumb and forefinger, held high for all to see ...

"Thou mixture rank, of midnight weeds collected,
With Hecate's ban thrice blasted, thrice
infected,
Thy natural magic and dire property,
On wholesome life usurp immediately."

With a melodramatic flourish, the player-Lucianus twirled, knelt before the sleeping player-king, and poured the contents into the player-king's ear. The faux-liege convulsed, his face in anguish as he clasped the violated side of his head.

"He *poisons* him in the garden for his estate!" Hamlet announced, making certain that everyone present understood exactly what was happening. And as he continued his outburst, he pivoted on his heel and hip so that he came into full view of Claudius' face – a face frozen and stolid ... but not stolid enough to hide the rampant pacing of his breath! "The sleeper's name is Gonzago: The story is real, and written in choice Italian – you shall see now how *the murderer gets the love of Gonzago's wife!*"

Claudius held out for a moment or two longer, his teeth grinding as his jaws clenched, his fingers squeezing the arms of his throne until there was no blood left within them ...

... and then he shot to his feet, coming to rigid and full attention, ramrod straight far beyond any soldier at attention before his commanding officer.

"The king *rises*," Ophelia noted, her bewilderment and perplexity over Hamlet's behavior momentarily distracted.

Slowly, the rest of the audience realized that the King was standing, and they scrambled to follow suit. They all expected some announcement – perhaps a demand for his nephew, the Prince, to cease his outcries so that the play might continue – but none was forthcoming. The King of Denmark merely stood there, painfully erect and staring fixedly upon the players below.

"What," Hamlet whispered, so low that even Ophelia did not make out what he said, "frighted with false fire?"

Finally, the Queen broke the awkward silence. "How fares my lord?"

"Give over the play," Polonius suggested, trying to

regain his own composure.

Claudius swallowed hard, tried to speak, failed, swallowed again ... and managed to command in a raspy voice, "Give me ... give me some *light*. Away!"

The King then turned and marched away. Calls for "Lights!" echoed from multiple sources throughout the theatre, and Gertrude, Polonius, and the remainder of the royal entourage rushed after their departed liege.

Tempered mayhem ensued. The players – uncertain what exactly had gone wrong, but fearful that *they* were, somehow, to blame – scrambled backstage. The audience – uncertain as to why the King had departed, but clear that, if nothing else, the show was over – evacuated the theatre.

And in the midst of it all stood the Prince of Denmark, his hands on his hips as his only trusted friend fought against the tide to meet him before the stage.

" 'Why,' " Hamlet began when Horatio drew within spoken earshot, leaping onto the stage itself and striking a dramatic pose, " 'let the stricken deer go weep, the hart ungalled play; for some must watch, while some must sleep – so runs the world away.' If the rest of my fortunes go bad for me, would not *this*, sir, and a forest of plumes from tragic actors, with two French-styled rosettes on my decorated shoes, get me a partnership in a company of players?"

"Half a share of the company's profits," Horatio remarked.

"A *whole* one, I. 'For thou dost know, O Damon dear, This realm dismantled was of Jove himself; and now reigns here A very, very'... peacock."

"You might have rhymed," Horatio noted with a smirk.

Hamlet barked a raucous laugh, then slid down from the stage and took his friend by the hands. "Oh, good Horatio, I'll take the ghost's word for a thousand pounds! Did you *see* it?!"

"Very *well*, my lord."

"Upon the talk of the poisoning?"

"I did *very* well note him."

"Ah, ha!" He called out to the now-empty theatre around them. "Come, some music! Come, the flutes! 'For if the king like not the comedy, Why then, belike, he likes it not, perdy.' Come, some music!"

He danced around Horatio, in what Horatio perceived as a forced little jig. How long it would have gone on, he would never know, as the Prince stopped when Rosencrantz and Guildenstern reentered the theatre.

"Good my lord," Guildenstern called as they approached, "may I have a word with you?"

"Sir, a whole *history*."

"The King, sir—"

"Aye, sir, what of him?"

"—is in his retirement marvelously *out of humor*."

"With *drink*, sir?"

Guildenstern drew a strengthening breath before continuing, "*No*, my lord, rather with *anger*."

"Your wisdom should show itself more richer to signify this to his *doctor*; for, for *me* to put him to his purging would perhaps plunge him into far *more* anger."

"*Please*, my lord ... put your discourse into some sensible form, and start not so wildly from my meaning."

Hamlet sighed gracelessly, rolling his eyes toward Horatio but for all three to see. "I am tame, sir. Speak."

Satisfied for the moment, Guildenstern pressed on with his business. "The Queen, your mother – in most great affliction of spirit – has sent me to you."

"You are welcome."

"*No*, my good lord, this courtesy is not genuine. If you would be so kind to give me a sincere answer, I will do your mother's commandment – if *not*, your permission to depart and my return shall be the end of my business."

"Sir ... I cannot."

Guildenstern glanced over at Rosencrantz, who seemed equally confused. Still, Rosencrantz decided to at least *try* and help. "You cannot ... *what*, my lord?"

"Give you a sincere answer – my wit is *diseased*! But, sir, such answer as I *can* give, you shall command ... or, rather, as you say, my mother. Therefore no more, but to the matter: My mother, you say ...?"

"Then she says this: Your behavior has struck her into bewilderment and wonder."

Hamlet clasped his hands before him, holding them just under his chin like an effeminate child. "Oh, wonderful son, that can so astonish a mother! But is there no sequel at the heels of this mother's admiration? Impart it."

"She desires to speak with you in her private chamber, before you go to bed."

Hamlet nodded. "I shall obey, were she ten times my mother. Have you any further business with me?"

Rosencrantz seemed sincerely hurt by the abrupt behavior and dismissal. "My lord," he spoke in a lower, less formal voice, "you once loved my friendship."

"So I do still, by these picking and stealing hands." He waggled his fingers.

"*Please*, my lord ... what is the cause of your distemper? You do, surely, bar the door upon your own freedom of action, if you deny your griefs to your friend."

"Sir ... I lack advancement."

Rosencrantz blinked, then shook his head in confusion. "How can that *be*," he reasoned, "when you have the public-given word of the King himself for your succession in Denmark?"

Hamlet smirked, "Aye, but sir, 'While the grass grows, the steed starves'... the proverb is somewhat stale." At that point, from off stage-left, some of the younger players – the recorder players – crept out to see what was happening. Hamlet saw them and, much to their surprise, rushed forward. "Oh, the recorders! Let me see one." He took the wooden flute from one of them, then ushered them away.

Skipping back to the stage's edge, he then gestured Guildenstern forward. "A private word with you ..." Twirling the flute through his fingers, he considered it as he ambled around to place his arm upon Guildenstern's shoulder. Lowering his voice, he asked, "Why do you go about to take advantage of me, as if you would drive me into a snare?"

Guildenstern shook his head. "Oh, my lord, if my duty is too bold, my love is too unmannerly."

Hamlet shook his own head and took a step away. "I do not understand *that* well at all." He offered the recorder. "Will you play upon this pipe?"

Guildenstern looked at the wooden instrument in confusion. "My lord, I cannot."

"I implore you."

"Believe me, I can*not*."

"I do beseech you."

Guildenstern sighed in frustration. "I have no such skill, my lord."

Hamlet *tsked*. "Come now – it is as easy as *lying*."

Guildenstern froze. Rosencrantz – who had indeed been listening as well he could from a few paces away – took a step backward ... only to feel Horatio's hand holding him in place.

"Govern these holes with your fingers and thumbs," the Prince continued, demonstrating upon the flute, "give it breath with your mouth, and it will discourse most eloquent music. Look here, these are the stops ..."

"But I cannot command these to any utterance of harmony," Guildenstern whined tightly. "I have *not* the skill."

At that, Hamlet threw the flute at Guildenstern, who yelped and knocked it aside a split-second before it struck him in the face. Rosencrantz made another attempt to retreat, and was once again halted by Hamlet's true friend.

"Why, look you now," the Prince shouted, "how unworthy a thing you make of *me*! You would play upon *me*; you would seem to know *my* stops; you would pluck out the heart of *my* mystery; you would sound *me* from my lowest note to the top of my range of voice – and there is much music, excellent voice, in *this* little instrument ... yet you cannot make it speak." He seized Guildenstern's right lapel and jerked him forward. "Christ's blood, do you think *I* am easier to be played on than a *pipe*?! Call me what instrument you will, though you can finger me ... you - cannot - *play* - upon - me."

Much to Guildenstern's relief, the tense moment was

broken by the entrance of the Lord Chamberlain. Hamlet stared into Guildenstern's eyes a moment longer ... then suddenly smiled, turned to the approaching Chamberlain, and called happily, "God bless you, sir!"

"My lord," Polonius announced, oblivious to the scene he had interrupted, "the Queen would speak with you, at once."

Hamlet rushed to him excitedly, then turned and pointed up to the perfectly plain, undecorated ceiling. "Do you see yonder cloud that's almost in the shape of a camel?"

Wearily, Polonius agreed, "By the mass, and it is like a camel, indeed."

But Hamlet appeared to reconsider. "I think it is like a weasel."

"It is backed like a weasel."

"Or like a whale?"

Now it was Polonius' turn to grind his teeth together. "Very like a whale."

Satisfied with his fun at the Chamberlain's expense, Hamlet said, "Then I will come to my mother at once." He gestured to the students. "*They* make me play the fool to the limit of my endurance. I will come by and by."

"I will say so," Polonius nodded, hastening to leave.

" 'By and by' is easily said," Hamlet called after him, before at last turning to his company and ordering, "Leave me, friends."

Guildenstern and Rosencrantz were more than happy to comply; Horatio notably less so. But soon enough, the Prince found himself alone upon the stage.

It is now the very witching time of night, when spells are cast, when churchyards yawn and Hell itself breathes

out contagion to this world. **Now** *I could drink hot blood,
and do such bitter business as the day would quake to look
on.* **Soft!** *– now to my mother.* **Oh,** *heart, lose not your
natural affections; never let the soul of murderous Nero
enter this firm bosom – let me be* cruel, *not unnatural: I will
speak daggers to her, but use none; my tongue and soul in
this be hypocrites; how in my words soever she be rebuked,
to never confirm them by making words into deeds, my soul,
consent!*

Indeed, he would visit his mother. But he had one other
bit of business to attend to first, one other family member to
whom he would pay sweet, dark tribute.

He would see Gertrude soon enough.

But now he would see *Claudius* ...

Part Three
Chapter Three

The door to the King's private chambers thundered open, and Claudius rolled into the room like a storm. Rosencrantz and Guildenstern followed tentatively behind him.

"I do *not* like his behavior," Claudius continued his controlled rant, "nor is it safe for us to allow his madness to freely roam. Therefore, prepare yourselves;" he moved to his desk, producing paper and quill and ink, "I will prepare your commission at once, and he shall go along with you to England: The nature of my position may not endure hazards so dangerous as are growing *hourly* out of his lunacies."

"We will provide ourselves," Guildenstern assured him. "It is most holy and religious caution to keep those many bodies safe that live and feed upon your majesty."

Rosencrantz chimed in, "The individual and private life is bound – with all the strength and armor of the mind – to keep itself from harm ... but much *more* that spirit upon whose welfare depends and rests the lives of *many*. The decease of majesty dies not alone, but, like a whirlpool, draws what's near it with it – it is like Fortune's wheel, fixed on the summit of the highest mount, to whose huge spokes ten thousand lesser things are fixed and adjoined ... which, when it falls, each small annexment, petty consequence, accompanies the boisterous descent. The King never did sigh alone, but with a general groan."

Claudius, who had only been listening with half-an-ear

from the beginning of their proclamations, snapped, "I pray you, *prepare* yourselves, to this speedy voyage ... for we will put *fetters* upon this fear, which now goes about too freely."

Rosencrantz glanced at Guildenstern, who nodded – they'd paid more than enough tongue tribute to their liege. "We will hasten."

Together, they rushed from the room, just as Polonius passed them on his way in.

"My lord," the Lord Chamberlain announced, "he's going to his mother's chambers. I'll hide myself behind the hanging arras, to hear their exchange; and I imagine she'll thrash him thoroughly – and, as you said, and wisely was it said, it is good that some audience *more* than a mother, since nature makes them partial to their sons, should *also* overhear the speech." He clapped himself on the chest, "Fare you well, my liege – I'll call upon you before you go to bed, and tell you what I know."

Through it all, Claudius was barely able to hold his tongue, to reign in his impatience and avoid screaming at the doddering old fool to get out of his sight. He needed to be alone – couldn't they *see* that?!

Instead, he managed a tight smile and said, "Thanks, my dear lord."

The endearment puffed Polonius up like a silly-looking pigeon ... but at least he finally turned and left.

As soon as the door closed, Claudius nearly collapsed across his desk. He set aside the quill with a hand far too shaky to write, and leaned back instead, his eyes closed and his breath quick and short. To have seen those ... those *things* that his damned nephew had reenacted on stage, for any and all to witness and judge ... it was too much ... too much ...

Oh, my offence is rank – it smells to Heaven! It has the primeval, eldest curse upon it, that which God struck upon Cain ... a brother's murder ...

Whimpering so softly even he could not hear himself – and therefore left unaware that it was even happening – he clasped his hands before him ... then sobbed and pulled his fingers apart.

I cannot pray, though my desire is as sharp as my resolve – my stronger guilt defeats my strong intent. And, like a man committed to double business, I stand in pause where I shall first begin, and therefore neglect both.

He opened his eyes and stared through the emotional mist upon his impotent hands.

What if this cursed hand were thickened with my brother's blood? Is there not rain enough in the sweet heavens to wash it white as snow? What purpose does mercy serve but to confront the visage of sin? And what's in prayer but this two-fold force, to be frozen in anticipation whenever we come to fall ... or pardoned being down?

Trying anew, he forced his hands to couple once more, his forehead tensing in desperate determination.

Then I'll look up; my fault is past. But, oh, what form of prayer can serve my turn? "Forgive me for my foul murder?" That cannot be; since I am still in possession of those fruits for which I did the murder: My crown, my own ambition, and my Queen. May one be pardoned ... and yet still retain the bounty of the offence? In the corrupted currents of this world, offence's bribing hand may shove by justice, and it is seen that the reward of vice itself often corrupts the law ... but it is not so in Heaven above; there is no trickery, there *the action lies in his true nature; and we ourselves are compelled, to face our very faults, to give in evidence.*

Sighing, his head sagged low, and he once again began to sob under his breath.

What *then?! What remains?! Try what repentance can. What can it not? Yet what can it when one cannot* repent?

"Oh, wretched state!" he spoke aloud, rising shakily to his feet. "Oh, bosom black as death! Oh, trapped soul, that – struggling to be free – is more entangled!"

Nearly stumbling, he found his way to an alcove near the far corner, an alcove arranged when his brother reigned, and which he himself had barely been able to look upon.

It was a simple grotto: A cushion upon which to kneel ... and a cross before which to pray.

"Help, angels! Make appraisal! Bow, stubborn knees; and, heart with strings of steel, be soft as sinews of the newborn babe! All may be well ... I pray ..."

Genuflecting at last, he fell silently into prayer, only the remaining ghost of his sobs drifting through the now-silent chamber.

That silence worked against the Prince of Denmark ... but it did not stop him.

Slithering through the barest gap of a side aperture, Hamlet gripped the hilt of his sword tightly. Sweat had crept upon his brow, and his body felt oily and taut.

It did not matter. He had seen enough. Finally, *finally*, he knew that he could take the ghost at its word. His reprehensible uncle's reaction to the Players' dramatization had been more damning than the loudest confession:

Claudius had murdered his father.

He would remain inactive no more; he would skulk and prance and feign madness no longer. Judgment was at hand, and by God, it would take place by *his* hand.

Slowly, softly, he advanced upon the self-absorbed, unsuspecting King.

Now *might I do it nicely,* now *while he is praying ... and* now *I'll do it! And so he goes ... he goes ... to Heaven...?*

Hamlet froze, his hand poised to draw his sword and divorce his uncle's head from his neck.

And this *is how I am revenged? This must be carefully considered: A villain kills my father ... and for that, I, his sole son, do send this same villain to* Heaven*?!*

Damn it all, the man was *praying*! It was as though all the Fates had decreed to torment him! He at last confirms his uncle's guilt ... and now his *perfect* opportunity (for how often would he be able to reach the Sovereign of Denmark without defense, without witness to stay his hand?) ... and the man was kneeling in prayer, beseeching his soul to God and Christ above.

Hamlet gritted his teeth, but, very slowly, his fingers relaxed their grip upon his sword's hilt.

Oh, this would be a reward*, not revenge. He took my father in a grossly, spiritually unprepared state – without the opportunity to fast; with all his sins in full bloom, as vigorous in May – and now who knows how his account stands, save Heaven ... but to the best of our knowledge and belief, it is heavy with him. Am I then revenged, to take Claudius during the purging of his soul, when* he *is fit and seasoned for his passage to God's graces?* No!

His hand finally slipped from his weapon, but instead of falling to his side, he began stroking the hilt lightly with his fingertips.

Stay in your sheath, sword, and be drawn at a more horrid time: When he is drunk asleep, or in his rage ... or in the incestuous pleasure of his bed; at gaming, swearing, or about some act that has no trace of salvation in it ... then trip him, *that his heels may kick at Heaven, and that his soul may be as damned and black as hell, whereto it goes.*

His decision made – much to his frustration – he carefully withdrew the way he had come in, his uncle never to know how close Death had come.

My mother waits ... and this medicine only prolongs *your sickly days.*

With that, he was gone.

A few minutes later, Claudius arose. He wiped the tears from his cheeks with the heel of his palms and straightened, crossing himself forehead to stomach and chest to chest.

"My words fly up, but my thoughts remain below – words without thoughts never to Heaven go."

PART THREE
CHAPTER FOUR

Holding her flowing gowns up so that she could walk with a faster stride, Gertrude entered her personal suites. And, trying her patience more than he knew, Polonius followed closely at her heels.

"He will come straight away," the Lord Chamberlain prattled on. "See that you chastise him *thoroughly*: Tell him that his pranks have been too irrepressible to bear, and that your grace has screened and withstood much anger on his behalf." Then he touched her hand in what he probably thought was a reassuring measure, and gestured toward one of several tapestries. "I'll withdraw in silence. Pray you, speak plainly with him."

From the outer hallway, Hamlet's teasing voice echoed, "Mother! ... Mother! ... Mother!"

Gertrude waved Polonius away, her equanimity slipping. "I'll warrant you, have no fear. Now *withdraw* – I hear him coming."

Nodding as though his neck were too loose upon his shoulders, Polonius stepped away at last and disappeared behind the decorative arras he had indicated.

And not a moment too soon, as the doors again swung inward – *burst* inward, in this case – and Hamlet actually *skipped* his way into the room. "Now, Mother," he asked with exaggerated glee, "what's the matter?"

Gertrude had had more than enough of this bizarre conduct. Drawing herself up, she snapped, "Hamlet, you have very much *offended* your father!"

In a heartbeat, Hamlet's impish smile vanished. He stood rock still, and his voice dropped an octave as he replied, "Mother ... *you* have much offended my father."

Gertrude was startled by the sudden and unexpected shift in his demeanor, but she was determined not to lose control of this conversation. "Come, come! You answer with a foolish tongue."

"Go, go," he returned, taking a step toward her, "you question with a *wicked* tongue."

She thrust her fists to her hips. "Why, how now, Hamlet!"

"What's the matter now?"

"Have you *forgotten* me?"

"No, by the cross, not so." His voice now dripped venom as he sidled ever closer to her. "You are the Queen, your husband's brother's wife. And – if only it were not so! – you are my *mother*."

Gertrude was nearly speechless. Since the death of his father, and her remarriage to her new husband, she had seen Hamlet in many forms: Aggrieved, willful, disoriented, deranged ... but she was unprepared for the *hatred* that she now saw in his eyes. "No, then..." She looked away from him, from those hate-filled eyes. "I'll set those to you that can speak ..." She moved around him, heading toward the door.

Hamlet uncoiled like a serpent. He seized her shoulders and drew her – and not gently – back into the center of the room. "Come, come, and sit you down; you shall not budge!" Turning, he propelled her backward so that she stumbled into a nearby chair. "You will not go until I have set you up a mirror where you may see the innermost part of yourself."

Gertrude gasped, "What will you *do*? You will not murder me?" But the heat in her son's damned eyes offered no reassurance, and she called out, "Help, help, ho!"

From behind the tapestry, Polonius heard her cry, and responded. But he was neither young nor fit enough to engage the Prince himself, and so he repeated her shout at the top of his own lungs. "What, ho! Help, help, help!"

Hamlet spun, his sword in his hand without a conscious decision to draw it. The voice, a man's, in his mother's chamber, hiding like a villain ...!

Hamlet did not know *how* Claudius had beaten him here, but it did not matter. He had hesitated before, but the miscreant was no longer praying, was he?

"How now!" he called, rushing to the moving tapestry. "A rat? Dead, I'd wager a ducat – *dead*!"

His sword pierced the fabrics and struck home. He felt it enter the targeted flesh, and gave it a fierce twist for good measure.

The figure spun away, wrapping itself up with the tapestry in the process. As the blood began to flow, a harsh whisper escaped – "Oh, I am slain!" – and then the man collapsed.

Hamlet froze, his sword pulling free as the body hit the floor. In the heat of the moment, he had been so *certain* that the voice that had called out had belonged to his uncle. But now ... that whisper did not sound right ... it sounded more like ... like ...

Gertrude crept forward, her hands covering her mouth in horror. "Oh, my ... what have you done?"

"I do not know," Hamlet admitted. "Is it the King?"

"Oh, what a rash and bloody deed this is ..."

" 'A bloody deed!' " he repeated, some of his former steel returning to his voice. "*Almost* as bad, good Mother, as kill a King and marry with his brother."

Gertrude stared at him, her eyes like moons. "As ... 'as *kill* a King?' "

"Aye, lady, that was my word." Reaching down, Hamlet jerked away the cloth to discover the late Lord Chamberlain staring unseeingly up at him. His suspicion confirmed, he shook his head. "You wretched, rash, intruding fool ... farewell. I mistook you for your better. But take your fortune: You have found that to be too meddlesome is a dangerous thing indeed."

Glancing up, Hamlet looked again to his mother, who gaped at the dead Polonius, her hands gripping, releasing, and gripping one another again. He stood and seized her by the arm.

"Enough wringing of your hands: Peace!" Turning about, he threw her onto her bed. "Sit down, and let *me* wring your *heart* – for so I shall, *if* it is still made of penetrable stuff, if the habit of constant ill-doing has not hardened it like brass, so that it is armored and fortified against all feeling."

Gertrude began to weep. "What have I *done*, that you dare speak so *rudely* against me?"

"Such an act that blurs the grace and blush of modesty, that calls virtue 'hypocrite,' takes off the rose from the fair forehead of an innocent love and sets a brand of shame there, and makes marriage-vows as false as gamblers' oaths! Oh, such a deed as plucks the very soul from the body of the marital contract, and sweet, sacred vows makes a jumble of words. Heaven's face blushes! And, oh, this Earth – with sad visage, as if for Judgment Day – is thought-sick at the act."

"Aye me, *what* act," Gertrude demanded, some of her self-righteous fire flickering like soft embers in the ashes of her son's rage, "that roars so loud, and thunders in the prelude?"

In an instant, Hamlet snatched something from her bed-table. At the same time, his other hand stole its way under his shirt at the throat. A moment later, he was kneeling on the bed over his mother, a silver locket and gold locket in each grasp.

"Look here, upon this picture," he snapped open the gold locket, "and on this," and then the silver, "the painted likeness of two brothers." He shook first the gold, the one containing the semblance of his true father. "See, what a grace was seated on this brow; the sun god Hyperion's curls; the forehead of Jove himself; an eye like the war god Mars, to threaten and command; a poise like the herald Mercury new-lighted on a Heaven-kissing hill." He sighed, staring upon the image with tears glistening in his eyes; in truth, Gertrude's own eyes were no longer dry. "A combination and a form indeed, where every god did seem to set his seal, to give the world assurance of a man: *This was your husband.*"

He lowered the gold locket ... and raised the silver, as though presenting the carcass of decayed vermin. "Look you *now*, what follows: Here is your *new* husband; like a mildewed ear of wheat, blasting his wholesome brother." He shook his head in sincere disbelief. "Have you *eyes*? Could you on *this* fair mountain leave to feed, and gorge on *this* barren moor? Ha! *Have you eyes*? You cannot call it love; for at your age the excitement in the blood is tame, it's humble, and waits upon the judgment ... and what judgment would step from *this* to *this*?"

Hamlet leaned in closer, and his breath was hot upon the tears on Gertrude's cheeks.

"The five senses, sure you have, or else you could not have motion ... but sure, those senses are paralyzed; for madness itself would not make such an error, nor could the senses be so enthralled into ecstasy but they would still reserve *some* quantity of choice, to serve in such a difference. What devil was it that thus has cheated you at blindman's bluff? Eyes without feeling, feeling without sight, ears without hands or eyes, smelling without all ... or but a sickly part of one true sense could not be so dazed."

He shook the two lockets in her face once more, his voice rising.

"Oh, *shame*, where is thy blush?! Oh, rebellious *Hell*, if thou can so rise in mutiny in a matron's bones ... then let virtue be as wax to flaming youth, and melt in her own fire; then proclaim *no* shame when the compulsive fervor gives the command, since frost itself burns as actively and reason panders to the gratification of will."

To Gertrude, "melt in her own fire" was the phrase of the moment. For she had surely shriveled away before her son's words. Words that had touched the deep, secret place within her own heart, words which rang awful and hurtful ... and true.

"Oh, Hamlet," she whispered, pleading, "speak no more: You have turned my eyes into my very soul ... and there I see such black and ingrained spots that will not lose their color."

But Hamlet would not relent – if anything, the plea drove him to greater passion. "No, but to live in the rank sweat of a greasy bed, stewed in corruption, talking sweetly, and making love over the nasty sty—!"

"Oh, speak to me no more!" Gertrude tried to cover his lips with her trembling fingers. "These words enter my ears like *daggers*. No more, sweet Hamlet!"

"A murderer and a villain," her son continued, now shaking her by the shoulders, "a slave that is not a *twentieth* part of the *tenth* of your former lord; a buffoon of kings; a pickpocket of the empire and the rule, that from a shelf stole the precious crown, and put it in his pocket!"

"No more!" Gertrude screamed, now trying to cover her ears instead. But Hamlet was shaking her so hard!

"A clownish king of shreds and patches—!"

And with those last words, Hamlet froze, his every muscle locking as rigid as that of a monument of diamond. Only his tongue continued to move and his throat to work, though no further sound escaped him.

For a brief moment, Gertrude feared that he had simply ranted until he had *broken* something inside, either his mind or his body. But then she realized that his bulging eyes were not simply gawking in paralysis, but actually appeared to be focusing upon something, something behind her.

Turning as best she could – for though he was no longer shaking her, Hamlet's fingers still dug fiercely into her arms – Gertrude tried to see what in the world had so stunned her raging son ...

Nothing. Nothing but the empty doorway. Hamlet was gaping at *nothing*.

But *Hamlet* did not see nothing. Oh, no. For him, the doorway was far from "empty." In the doorway, Hamlet once more saw the visage of his deceased father, dressed now not in his armor of state, but in his simple nightgown, as though he had just finished his evening toddy and decided to retire.

But the look. Oh, the look! The *accusation* in those eyes!

"Save me," Hamlet whispered at last, his voice tight and dry, "and hover over me with your wings, you Heavenly guards." Swallowing hard, he addressed the spirit which glared at him so. "What would your gracious figure have of me ...?"

"Alas," Gertrude also whispered, staring up at her son once more, "he's *mad*."

"Do you not come to chide your tardy son," Hamlet continued to address the spirit only he could see, "that, fretting away time and energy, lets go by the urgent passion of your dread command? Oh, speak!"

The shade speared its son with eyes of ice ... and granted his wish. *"Do not forget,"* it commanded. *"This visitation is but to whet your almost blunted purpose. But, look, utter bewilderment sits upon your mother – oh, step between her and her fighting soul. Imagination in the weakest bodies works the strongest. Speak to her, Hamlet."*

Treading carefully upon unsure ground, Hamlet turned and asked his mother is a rasping voice, "How are you, lady?"

The Queen gaped at the Prince. "Alas, how are *you*, that you turn your eye upon nothingness and hold discourse with the incorporeal air? Furthermore, your eyes peep with

HAMLET: PRINCE OF DENMARK 149

wildly spirits, and – as the sleeping soldiers upon the sudden call to arms – your smoothly brushed hair, like dead tissue come alive, starts up and stands on end!" Gently, cautiously, she reached up to caress his cheek. "Oh, gentle son, sprinkle cool self-control upon the heat and flame of your distemper. At what do you look?"

"At him, at him!" Hamlet wheezed insistently. "Look, how pale he glares! His appearance and words, united preaching to stones, would make them responsive. Do not look upon me," he said to the ghost only he could see, "lest with this piteous action you alter my purposeful deeds – then what I have to do will lack proper character; tears perchance for blood."

This time Gertrude was more aggressive with her son, taking him by the shoulders and shaking him. "To *whom* do you speak this?"

Hamlet looked at her, at the ghost, and then back to her again. "Do you see ... *nothing* there?"

"*Nothing* at all. That," she gestured around the empty room – the doorway, the walls, the trappings, "is all I see."

"Nor did you *hear* nothing?"

"*No* ... nothing but ourselves."

The ghost burned one more meaningful glance at Hamlet, and then made to retreat, a move that combined the reality of leaving the room with the impossibility of fading from sight.

"Why, look you there!" Hamlet rose to his knees, now kneeling upon the bed as though in prayer. "Look, how it steals away! My father, in his nightdress as when he lived! Look, where he goes, even now, out at the portal!"

At the last moment, it occurred to Hamlet to follow the

ghost, as he had the night of their first meeting those months ago ...

... but it was too late. The spirit of his father was gone.

"This is the very coinage of your brain," Gertrude spoke to him, once more treading guardedly. "This bodiless creation is very cunning in madness."

"Madness!" he scoffed, though with little force. "My pulse, as yours, keeps time temperately, and makes as healthful music. It is *not* madness that I have uttered. Bring me to the test, and I will repeat the matter word-for-word; an ability from which madness would skip away."

Softening, he took Gertrude's hands in his own, and for the first time in many, many months, he spoke to her as a son.

"Mother," he pleaded, "for love of God, do *not* lay that soothing salve to your soul, telling yourself that it is not your trespass, but my 'madness' which speaks. It will but skin and film the ulcerous place, all the while rank corruption, undermining all within, infects unseen. *Confess* yourself to Heaven, *repent* what is past, *avoid* what is to come, and do not spread the excrement on the weeds, to make them *ranker* than they already are. Forgive me this, my virtue ... for in the grossness of these gluttonous times, virtue itself must beg pardon of vice, yea, bow and entreat for leave to do vice good."

"Oh, Hamlet," she cried, the tears flowing freely now, "you have cleft my heart in two."

"Oh, *throw away* the worser part of it, and live the *purer* with the other half. I'll bid you good night ... but do *not* go to my uncle's bed – *assume* a virtue, if you do not have it." He squeezed her hand tighter. "*Refrain* tonight ...

and that shall lend a kind of easiness to the *next* abstinence, the next even *more* easy. For habit can almost change the stamp of nature: Either lodge the Devil, or throw him out with wondrous potency."

He held her gaze until, at last, she nodded her agreement. He kissed the back of her hand and stood. "Once more, good night. And when you desire to be repentant and blessed, I'll beg forgiveness of you. For this same lord," he indicated Polonius, "I do repent: But Heaven has pleased it so, to punish me with this and this with me, that I must be their agent of justice. I will dispose of him, and will answer for the death I gave him." He sighed. "So ... again, good night. I must be cruel, only to be kind – thus bad begins and worse remains to come." Hamlet bent over the Lord Chamberlain's still form, hesitated, then straightened and turned to her yet again. "*One* more word, good lady."

Exhausted, she asked, "What shall I do?"

"*Not this*, by *no* means: Do *not* let the bloated King tempt you again to bed; nor pinch wantonly on your cheek; nor call you his mouse; and do *not* let him, for a pair of filthy kisses or fondling your neck with his damned fingers, make you to frazzle all this matter out ... that I, in my essence, am *not* in madness, but I only *act* mad."

The Queen's eyes widened ... and then she nodded in understanding that almost, but did not quite, shock her.

"It was good you let him know," he continued, "for who but a *Queen* – fair, sober, wise – would from a *toad*, from a *bat*, a *tom-cat*, hide such dear matters of intense concern? Who would do so? No, in despite of sense and secrecy, open the door of the cage on the house's top. Let the birds fly, and – like the famous ape – to try experiments, in the basket creep, and break your own neck in the fall."

The Queen nodded again, this time more assertively. "Be assured: If words are made of breath, and breath of life ... then I have *no life* to breathe what you have said to me."

Hamlet, visibly relieved, smiled at her briefly before the light again fell from his face. "I must go to England; you know that?"

Gertrude started. "Alas, I had forgotten – it has been so decided."

"There's letters sealed, and my two schoolfellows – whom I will trust as I would fanged adders – they bear the command; they must escort me, and marshal me to some knavish scheme against me. Let it work, for it is the sport to have the engineer blown up by his own explosives – and it shall be hard going, but I will delve one yard below their mines, and blow them to the moon."

Now Hamlet again bent over Polonius. "Oh, it is most sweet, when in one line two crafts directly meet. This man shall send me packing – I'll lug the corpse into the neighboring room. Mother, good night. Indeed this counselor is now most still, most secret and most grave, who was in life a foolish, prattling knave."

He slipped his hands under the other's armpits, and began dragging the body. "Come, sir, let's finish my conversation with you. Good night, Mother."

As Gertrude watched in exhausted angst, her son, with his cumbersome cargo in tow, backed through the doorway and disappeared into the darkness beyond.

PART THREE
CHAPTER FIVE

King Claudius strode through the corridor toward his Queen's chambers. He may have had a terrible bout of compunction following his nephew's latest antics, but now that he had taken his private time, he felt more grounded – he would answer for his sins in the afterlife, and then *only* to the Lord, his God ... most certainly *not* to the reigning Prince of Denmark.

Ah, but "reigning" for how long ...?

Rosencrantz and Guildenstern followed closely behind, rushing to keep up with their liege.

"There's hidden substance to these sighs," he said to them just as they reached his destination, continuing his previous tread of thought for these two simple but useful lackeys, "these exaggerated heaves of breath that Hamlet releases for our benefit. You must decipher their meaning – it is necessary that we understand them."

He entered the room and addressed his wife without preamble. "Where is your son?"

Gertrude did not answer immediately. Instead, she commanded the two students, "Leave us alone here a little while."

Rosencrantz and Guildenstern exchanged a puzzled glance, but only briefly. They withdrew in reasonable haste.

Only when they were alone did Gertrude speak to her husband, "Ah, my good lord, what have I seen tonight!"

"*What*, Gertrude?" Claudius demanded, concern once again threatening his confidence. "How is Hamlet?"

Gertrude released a short laugh at that, but it rang more of tears than of joy. "*Mad* as the sea and wind, when both clash for which is the mightier. In his unruly fit, he hears something stir behind the arras, whips out his rapier, cries, 'A rat, a rat!' and, in this crazy notion, kills the unseen good old man ... Polonius."

With that, she gestured across the room to the streaked, bloody mess that decorated her floor like some dark vision elicited from the Devil's own brush.

Claudius gasped, his knees nearly giving way as the breath threatened to leave him altogether. Not Polonius! But the *implications* behind such a blind-eyed murder shook him even further.

"Oh, grievous deed!" he whispered. "If I had been there instead, it would have been the same with *me*. His freedom is full of threats to us all – to you, to me, to *everyone*." He shook his head. "Alas, how shall this bloody deed be accounted for to the people? It will be laid to *me* as King, whose foresight should have kept the mad young man tethered, restrained, and out of others' company ... but so much was my love, I could not understand what was most fit – but, like the owner of a foul disease, to keep it secret ... I let it feed. Even on the vital essence of life."

He again shook his head, this time covering his eyes with shaking hands. All the doubt and angst he had *thought* to have conquered in prayer came rushing back with a vengeance.

No. This must not continue.

Lowering his hands, he stared down into Gertrude's moist eyes. "Where has he gone?"

"To do away with the body he has killed. Over whom

his very madness, like some vein of gold among a mine of lesser metals, shows itself pure – he *weeps* for what is done."

At this, Claudius scoffed, "Oh, Gertrude, come away! The sun shall no sooner touch the mountains than we will ship him away hence – and, with all our majesty and skill, we must both permit and excuse this vile deed." He turned, raising his voice. "Ho, Guildenstern!"

A scant heartbeat passed before the students rejoined them.

"Friends," he announced, "we require further aid of you both: Hamlet, in madness, has slain Polonius, and he has dragged him from his mother's room."

Rosencrantz's covered his mouth in shock; Guildenstern faired better, consigning his reaction to a thick swallow.

"Go seek him out," the King commanded, "speak courteously to him ... and bring the body into the chapel." When they merely stood there, he clapped his hands. "I pray you, make haste."

As they stumbled over one another to exeunt, he turned back to his Queen. "Come, Gertrude, we'll call upon our wisest friends, and let them know both what we mean to do, and what is untimely done. So that envious slander – whose whisper over the world's breadth, as straight as the cannon to its target, transports its poisoned shot – may miss our names, and hit the woundless air."

He took her hand, lifted it to his lips, and bestowed upon it a saddened kiss.

"Oh, come away," he whispered. "My soul is full of discord and dismay."

They left the blood-scented room.

PART THREE
CHAPTER SIX

Slipping out from the crevice behind and beneath the lobby staircase, Hamlet coughed dust from his lungs and wiped it from his hands.

Safely stowed.

He did not really believe that this little "hiding place" would conceal the body for any length of time. He merely wanted to delay the confrontation as long as possible, to unsettle it, to agitate and bewilder the whole situation. He had avoided a direct confrontation with Claudius this long only because the fratricidal bastard did, for now, wear the royal crown of Denmark ...

... but killing the Lord Chamberlain had not exactly been his wisest move, either. No, for now, he needed to play his "madness card" for all it was worth. It might be the only thing saving his life in very short order.

"Hamlet! Lord Hamlet!"

Very short order indeed.

"What noise? Who calls on Hamlet?" he called out innocently, although he had recognized the voice of Rosencrantz immediately. When the two students, ever the pair, entered, he forced a crafty smile. *Oh, here they come.*

When they drew near, Rosencrantz – with a surprisingly forceful tone that he usually left to Guildenstern – demanded, "What have you done, my lord, with the dead body?"

Hamlet made a show of considering his words. He

cocked his head to one side, placed his finger upon the tip of his bearded chin. Finally, he told them, "Compounded it with dust – 'Dust thou art, and unto dust shalt thou return'."

"Tell us where it is, that we may take and carry it to the chapel."

"Do not believe it."

Rosencrantz blinked in confusion. "Believe what?"

Guildenstern merely heaved a sigh.

"That I can keep *your* secrets and not mine *own*," Hamlet told him. "Besides, to be questioned by a sponge! What reply should be made by the son of a King?"

Rosencrantz's atypical fortitude returned. "You take me for a *sponge*, my lord?"

"Aye, sir," Hamlet said with a smile that slowly faded as he spoke, "that soaks up the King's favor, his rewards, his authority. But such officers do the King best service in the end. He keeps them, like an apple, in the corner of his jaw; first bitten, to be last swallowed – when he needs what you have gleaned, it is but squeezing you ... and, sponge, you shall be *dry* again."

Rosencrantz managed to hold Hamlet gaze while admitting, "I do not understand you, my lord."

"I am glad of it – a knavish speech is meaningless in a foolish ear."

"My lord, you *must* tell us where the body is, and go with us to the King."

"The body is with the King," Hamlet sing-songed, "but the King is not with the body. The King is a *thing*—"

"A '*thing*,' my lord!" Guildenstern interrupted, aghast.

"Of *nothing*." Then Hamlet shrugged, as though he had not a care in the world. "Bring me to him." Then he again sing-songed the cry of the common children's game of hide-and-seek, "Hide fox, and all after!"

Hamlet sauntered from the room, with Rosencrantz and Guildenstern in tow. Toward the King ...

... and away from Polonius' current resting place.

CHAPTER SEVEN

King Claudius paced to and fro before his desk. He had anticipated feeling more secure back in his own chambers, but this had proven not to be the case. Instead of providing a source of confidence, the discomfiting walls reminded him of his true hour of weakness earlier this very evening when, in his impotence, he had fallen on his knees before God.

So he brooded. And paced. And spoke at his surrounding attendants without really seeing them.

"I have sent his friends to seek him," he explained to no one in particular, "and to find the body. How dangerous is it that this man goes loose! Yet I must not put the strong law on him: He's loved by the irrational multitude who favor him, *not* in their judgment, but their *eyes* – and where it is so, the offender's *punishment* is weighed, but never the *offence*. To manage everything smoothly and equably, this sudden sending him away must seem judicially and fairly considered – diseases grown desperate are relieved by desperate remedy, or not at all."

The door opened, and a winded Rosencrantz entered. The King whirled upon him. "How now! What has befallen?"

"Where the dead body is bestowed, my lord, we cannot get from him."

"But where *is* he?"

Rosencrantz gestured to the still-open door. "Outside, my lord; guarded, to know your pleasure."

Claudius nodded his approval. "Bring him before me."

Rosencrantz stepped back and called over his shoulder, "Ho, Guildenstern! Bring in my lord."

Claudius' heart had scarcely beaten twice before his nephew appeared, with Guildenstern a half-step behind him. Hamlet appeared easy, smug – oh, how Claudius longed to strike that smirk from his lips!

But he took a calming breath and asked, "Now, Hamlet, where's Polonius?"

Hamlet quipped, "At supper."

" 'At supper!' *Where*?"

Hamlet seemed to consider this with great deliberation. "Not where he eats, but where he is *eaten*: A certain assembly of crafty worms are even now at him. Your worm is your only emperor, with respect to what it eats – we fatten all other creatures to fatten *us*, and we fatten *ourselves* for the maggots – your fat king and your lean beggar are but different courses of the same meal; two dishes, but to one table. That's the end."

Fed up, Claudius turned away from the frustrating young man and growled, "Alas, *alas*!" Perhaps Hamlet *wanted* to be killed, and therefore to martyr himself ... but to what cause? That made no sense, and yet Claudius could not fathom any other reason for these many ramblings, unless Hamlet were truly, deeply *mad* after all.

And still the Prince continued, "A man may fish with the worm that has eaten a king, and a cat of the fish that has fed on that worm."

Claudius *still* did not understand the point to this, but he knew that the constant use of the "king" metaphor did not sit well with him. "What do you mean by this?" he hissed.

"Nothing," Hamlet smiled, all innocence, "but to show you how a king may undertake a royal journey of state ... through the guts of a beggar."

Claudius stepped forward until he and Hamlet where nose-to-nose. He dropped his voice into his most commanding, *displeased* royal tone and repeated, "Where ... is ... *Polonius*?"

But Hamlet met the King's eye without flinching. "In Heaven; send someone hither to see ... and if your messenger does not find him *there*, then seek him in the *other* place *yourself*."

One of the attendants gasped openly, and Claudius saw Rosencrantz's fingertips rise as if by their own volition to cover his lips. Claudius simply could not accept such an insult, not when spat in his face before an audience of the court.

And perhaps Hamlet sensed that he had indeed taken things a step too far, because he suddenly returned to his lighter, nonchalant tone and, with a shrug, added, "But indeed, if you do not find him within a month, you shall *smell* him as you go up the stairs into the lobby."

Claudius looked away just long enough to order, "Go seek him there." Three of the attendants immediately rushed to obey.

Before they could make their clean exit, Hamlet called after them, "He will stay until you come."

Now Claudius stepped over to his desk and collected a sealed envelope. "Hamlet, this deed, for your special safety – which I hold with tenderness, just as I dearly grieve for what you have done – must send you hence, with fiery quickness. Therefore, prepare yourself: The boat is ready, and the wind is favorable, your associates await, and everything is prepared ... for England."

Hamlet gasped dramatically in clearly feigned surprise. "For England!"

"Aye, Hamlet."

Next the Prince smiled, "Good." As though it had been *his* idea all along.

"So is it, if you knew our purposes."

"*Heaven* sees them. But, come," he gestured to Rosencrantz and Guildenstern, "for England!" Hamlet plucked the envelope from Claudius' hand, waved it back and forth like a gaudy magician, and passed it to a dour Guildenstern. He then addressed the King once more. "Farewell, dear mother."

Claudius stiffened, and corrected, "Your loving *father*, Hamlet."

"My *mother*," the Prince insisted. "Father and mother is man and wife; man and wife is one flesh; and so ... *my mother*."

And then he shocked them all by kissing Claudius on the tip of his nose. Before anyone could react, he pirouetted and galloped from the room. "Come – for *England*!"

"Follow closely at his heels," Claudius growled at the recovering students, "tempt him with speed aboard – do not delay; I'll have him hence tonight: *Away*! For everything is sealed and done that otherwise relates to the affair. Pray you, make haste."

Guildenstern bowed deeply and departed; Rosencrantz merely tottered after him, his head still spinning from the rapid chain of events.

And, dear King of England, Claudius thought, *if you*

hold my love in any respect – as my great power may make you think upon it, since your scar yet looks raw and red after the Danish sword, and your fear compels you to pay homage to us – you may not disregard my sovereign command ... which imports at full, by these letters in accordance with that effect, the present death *of* Hamlet.

Do it, King of England, for he rages like an endless fever in my blood, and you must cure *me. Until I know it is done, however my fortunes my turn, my joys were never begun.*

Part Three
Chapter Eight

The wind moaned softly, but deeply, across the barren plane. The snow married with the dense fog to birth a white gulf that seemed to span both inches from the face and to eternity.

Through this, Prince Fortinbras of Norway led his steed and his First Captain, who in turn led his impressive army. A "militia" was the official designation in the eyes of his uncle ... but an *army* it was.

"Go, Captain," Fortinbras spoke in a barely audible rasp, "greet the Danish King for me; tell him that, by his licence, Fortinbras craves the escort for a promised march over his kingdom. You know the rendezvous. If that his majesty would aught with us, we shall pay our respects in his presence ... and let him know so."

The Captain nodded. "I will do it, my lord."

"Go slowly on." And Fortinbras fell into his characteristic silence, pulling on the reins and falling back slightly to take over the Captain's position. The Captain steered his own mount away, angling for the territory of mighty Elsinore.

Far sooner than he expected, the Captain spotted a compliment through the drifts of fog. An escort party, perhaps ...? But no, they were too early, too close, and too few in number.

As the Captain drew nearer, Hamlet – underdressed for the weather, but having little choice as he had been somewhat expedited from the royal grounds – wrenched his gaze from the grand horde marching through the tundra and called out, "Good sir, whose troops are these?"

The Captain commanded his mount to a halt. "They are of Norway, sir."

Hamlet considered this, even as Rosencrantz and Guildenstern stepped up alongside of him ... as though he might suddenly throw himself upon the Norwegian, seize the soldier's horse, and gallop away from their charge. "How purposed, sir, I pray you?"

"Against some part of Poland."

"Who commands them, sir?"

"The nephew to old Norway, Fortinbras."

Now this *really* gave Hamlet something to think about. It had been a short time since Claudius had patted himself on the back for having dealt with young Fortinbras so soundly. "Does it go against the *main* of Poland, sir, or for some frontier?"

At this, the Captain hesitated. When at last he spoke, it was with visible distaste. "To speak truthfully, and with no embellishment, we go to gain a little patch of ground that has in it no profit but the name. To pay annual rent of five ducats – *five* – I would not farm it; nor will it yield to Norway or the Pole a higher rate, should it be sold outright."

"Why, then ... the King of Poland never will defend it."

"*Yes*," the Captain corrected. "It is already garrisoned."

Rosencrantz and Guildenstern were puzzled, but Hamlet understood all too well. He shook his head in disgust. "Two thousand souls and twenty thousand ducats will not bring to a conclusion the question of this trifling matter – *this* is the festering boil of too much wealth and peace, that spreads its infection inward, and shows no external cause for why the man dies." He spat upon the ground.

Then, sighing, he forced a courteous smile and said, "I humbly thank you, sir."

The Captain nodded both his acceptance of thanks, and of his unspoken agreement with Hamlet's view of the repellent matter. "God be with you, sir," he said, and then led his steed away.

They stood there a minute longer before Rosencrantz finally cleared his throat in obvious fashion. "Will you please go, my lord?"

Hamlet rolled his eyes and grumbled, "I'll be with you straight away – go a little ahead of me."

The students again exchanged that worrisome glance. But, in the end, they obeyed the still-royal criminal and moved on, leaving the Prince to contemplate the passing army.

How all occasions do denounce me, and spur my dull revenge! What is a man, if his chief good and profit of his time be but to sleep and feed? A beast, *nothing more. Surely, He that made us with such large power of reasoning, looking before and after, did not give us that capability and god-like reason to whither within us* unused.

Now ... whether it is bestial forgetfulness, or some craven scruple of thinking too precisely *on the outcome – a thought which, divided, has but* one *part wisdom and ever* three *parts cowardice – I do not know why I still live to say "This thing's still undone." Since I have cause, and will, and strength, and* means *to do it. Examples as weighty as Earth exhort me: Witness this very army of such size and expanse, led by a delicate and tender prince, whose spirit –*

puffed with divine ambition – scorns the unforeseeable event, exposing what is mortal and unsure to all that fortune, death, and danger dare, even for an eggshell. Rightly to be great *is not to stir without great cause, but to find great quarrel in a trifle when* honor *is at stake.*

How, then, do I *stand, having a father killed, a mother stained, incentives of my reason and my blood ... and let all sleep? While, to my shame, I see the imminent death of twenty thousand men, that – for an illusion and deceit of fame – go to their graves like beds, fight for a plot of land which isn't large enough to allow the opposing armies to engage upon its soil, which has not enough tomb and receptacle to bury the slain?*

Oh, from this time forth, my thoughts be bloody ... or be *nothing worth!*

PART FOUR
CHAPTER ONE

The *screams*. The screams were the worst.

The sobbing was heart-aching, the tears were depressing, the rambling was, at best, irritating ... but the *screams* were fit to drive one as mad as she who loosed them upon the world.

Gertrude turned away from Horatio and the attendant, her stance firm.

"I will *not* speak with her," the Queen stated firmly. Didn't they understand? Didn't they know that she could not endure getting any closer to the source of those hellish screams?

The attendant with Horatio – a gentleman whose name she could not recall at the moment – drew a deep breath, and Gertrude knew that they would not leave her so easily.

"She is persistent," he explained, "indeed, out of her mind – her moods should be *pitied*."

Gertrude tamed a shiver that threatened to course through her as the screams again echoed through the chamber around them. "What does she *want*?"

Another glance at Horatio, then, "She speaks mostly of her father; says she hears there are deceptions in the world; she closes in, and beats her chest; takes grievous offence at the smallest trifle; speaks obscurely of things, that carry but half-sense – what she says is meaningless, yet the distracted manner of it does move the hearers to *try* and make sense of it; they guess at it, and patch the words up to fit their *own* thoughts ... the words, as her winks, and nods, and gestures yield them, indeed would make one think there might *be* thought, though not at all sure, yet very unhappy."

Now Horatio stepped forward, and the Queen turned to regard him. For the moment, the screams had stopped.

"It would be *good* if she were spoken with, for she may strew dangerous conjectures in ill-breeding minds."

Gertrude locked eyes with this young man, who had so befriended her dear, dear Hamlet ... but if she allowed her thoughts to tender that way, she herself might go mad even *without* the help of those awful screams. At last she said, "Let her come in."

Horatio bowed, turned, and strode from the room ... perhaps a little too swiftly, as though he feared his Lady would change her mind?

To my sick soul, as sin's true nature is, each trifle seems prologue to some great calamity – so full of foolish anxiety is guilt ... it spills itself in fearing to be spilt.

The far door reopened, and Horatio returned ... followed a heartbeat later by the deranged Ophelia.

The girl looked around, her arms clearly twitching beneath her restraining harness. "Where is the beauteous majesty of Denmark?" she asked.

Gertrude forced herself to step forward, to attempt a welcoming smile, but inside she feared the eruption of those screams she had heard for days now. "How now, Ophelia."

Ophelia glanced her way, briefly. Her head cocked to one side ... and then, to Gertrude's horrified bafflement, she began skipping – *skipping* – around the perimeter of the room.

Ophelia sang, "How should I your true love know

From another one?
By his cockle hat and staff,
And his sandal shoon."

Horatio and the gentlemen looked on helplessly. Gertrude swallowed heavily, then asked, "Alas, sweet lady, what imports this song?"

"Say you? Nay, pray you, mark:
He is dead and gone, lady,
He is dead and gone;
At his head a grass-green turf,
At his heels a stone."

Gertrude reached out, if in nothing else than in the hopes that she would cease her maddening *skipping*. "Nay, but, Ophelia—"

Ophelia *did* halt for a moment, turned on her in annoyance, and scolded, "Pray you, pay attention!" She then resumed her skipping, and her song went on.

"White his shroud as the mountain snow ..."

The rear chamber door opened, and Claudius entered. Gertrude hurried to him, gesturing to Ophelia as though perhaps *he* might offer some solution to her distraction.

"Alas," she whispered, "look here, my lord."

" ... Larded with sweet flowers
Which bewept to the grave did go
With true-love showers."

Claudius nodded to Gertrude, then lifted his voice. "How are you, pretty lady?"

Ophelia skidded to a halt once more. She turned, spied the King, and performed an awkward curtsey – "awkward" in that her arms were bound, and she was not wearing a dress to begin with. "*Well*, God reward you!" She then sort of scuttled forward, shuffling her feet and rocking her head side-to-side with exaggerated motion. When she drew near, she said in a conspiratorial voice, "They say the owl was a baker's daughter. Lord, we know what we are, but know not what we may be." Then she bellowed, "God be at your table!" causing both Claudius and Gertrude to start.

"Conceit upon her father," Claudius commented without breaking their eye-contact.

Ophelia smiled kindly. "Pray you, let's have no words of this; but when they ask you what it means, say you this:

To-morrow is Saint Valentine's day,
All in the morning betime,
And I a maid at your window,
To be your Valentine.
Then up he rose, and donn'd his clothes,
And dupp'd the chamber-door;
Let in the maid, that out a maid
Never departed more."

Claudius reached out to touch her sweaty hair. "Pretty Ophelia ..." he whispered in sorrow.

But the young girl drew back. "Indeed, la, without an oath, I'll make an end on it ..." She resumed her skipping and her song.

"By Gis and by Saint Charity,
Alack, and fie for shame!
Young men will do't, if they come to't;
By cock, they are to blame.
Quoth she, before you tumbled me,
You promised me to wed.
So would I ha' done, by yonder sun,
An thou hadst not come to my bed."

Suddenly depleted, Claudius turned to his wife. "How long has she been this way?"

Before Gertrude could reply, Ophelia skipped right up to them, barely avoiding colliding with the Queen as she did so. "I hope all will be well," she told them. "We must be patient – but I cannot choose but weep, to think they should lay him in the cold ground. My brother shall know of it, and so I thank you for your good counsel." Then she whirled, and hustled back to Horatio and the gentleman. "Come, my coach!" She then tilted her head back, and spun in circles on her way to the door Claudius had left open. "Good night, ladies; good night, sweet ladies; good night, good night ..."

And, with that, she was gone.

Gertrude could only thank Heaven that she had seen fit not to scream.

Claudius addressed Horatio. "Follow her closely; give her good watch, I pray you."

Horatio and the gentleman rushed to do his bidding.

Claudius unleashed a sigh from his deepest soul, his hands covering his eyes as he struggled to keep his voice calm.

"Oh, *this* is the poison of deep grief ... it springs all from her father's death." He allowed his hands to drop from his face, and turned toward his wife, although he still seemed to be staring more *past* her than *at* her. "Oh, Gertrude ... Gertrude ... when sorrows come, they come not as single scouts but in *battalions*. First, her father slain. Next, your son gone ... and he most *violent author* of his own justified removal. The people confused, thick and suspicious in their thoughts and whispers, for good Polonius' death – and we have done but *foolishly*, in secret and under haste to bury

him.   Poor Ophelia *divided* from herself and her fair
judgment, without which we are soulless, outward forms, or
mere beasts, to her."

Now, he *did* look directly upon her, and she did not find
the slightest comfort in his eyes. "And last, and as much
containing as all these ... her *brother*, Laertes, is coming
from France in secret; he feeds on his doubts, keeps himself
in gloom – away from the light of truth – and does not lack
gossipers to infect his ear with pestilent speeches of his
father's death ... speeches in which poverty, destitute of all
facts, will not hesitate to charge *me* with this crime in many
an ear." He reached for her hand. "Oh, my dear Gertrude,
this, like a cannon firing scattered charges, gives me, in many
places, *superfluous* death."

Gertrude stared at his out-stretched hand, hesitating.
She knew what was expected of her; she knew her lawfully-
wedded husband wanted some *comfort*. And yet ...

The decision – whatever it might have been – was taken
from her. A horrendous *crash* sounded throughout the
castle. Gertrude had lived here long enough to guess what it
might be: The gate, either unsecured or already partially ajar,
had been slammed fully open, the doors swinging back to
collide with the adjoining walls.

But ... *why* would that have happened ...? And were
those *voices* she now heard, voices raised in anger, in
rage...?

"Alas, what noise is this?"

Claudius shook his head, indicating that he, too, was
unsure. His reaction, however, was less stilted. "Where are
my Swiss guards?!" he called out in what Gertrude now
thought of as his "royal voice." He clapped his hands

sharply. "Let them guard the door!"

Another entree, opposite the door through which Ophelia had fled, opened to reveal a panting messenger. The way she stumbled into the chamber suggested that she had been running for some time.

"What is the matter?" Claudius demanded.

"*Save yourself*, my lord," the woman gasped, sending a chill through both members of the royal family. "The ocean, rising higher than its shores, does not eat the lands with more impetuous haste than young Laertes, in a riotous, rebellious advance, overpowers your officers. The rabble call him 'lord;' and, as if the world were now but to begin, antiquity forgotten, custom not known, the ratifiers and props of every pledge, they cry 'We choose – *Laertes* shall be *king*!' Caps, hands, and tongues, applaud it to the clouds: 'Laertes shall be king, Laertes king!' "

Yes, that *was* what they were calling! As the mob drew closer and closer to this relatively small chamber off from the royal hall, Gertrude heard that they were calling many things, but the cry for this prompt insurrection – the cry for Laertes – was the clearest. In spite of her recent ... "reservations" ... regarding her new husband, Gertrude was appalled. Had the people not accepted Claudius, embraced him? And now, following the upset call of the late Lord Chamberlain's son, they would turn on him like rabid dogs?!

"How cheerfully on the false trail they cry!" she snapped. She called out, ignoring the fact that they could not yet hear her. "Oh, you follow the *wrong scent*, you false Danish dogs!"

Another crash, much louder and nearer than the first – indeed, just outside this very chamber – shook the floor.

"The doors are broke," Claudius remarked, now surprisingly calm.

At last, the final set of doors collapsed inward. A mob of some two or three dozen, possibly more, crowded in the outer hallway. The messenger screamed and ran, her duty to her King apparently fulfilled in her eyes. Now Gertrude *did* take her husband's hand, pulling him after the messenger and away from the angry rabble.

To her shock and dismay, Claudius stood his ground.

"Where is this King?!" demanded a familiar voice. The crowd – which had ground to a halt some ten feet inside the room – parted, and Laertes emerged. He spotted the King in an instant, and raised his sword to point at Claudius' heart. "Sirs," he said, with satisfaction, to the men around him, "all of you, wait outside."

"No!" several of them grumbled.

"Let us come in!" another demanded.

"I pray you, give me *leave*!"

With that, the Danes begrudgingly nodded as a group and slowly, dolefully, withdrew, muttering, "We will, we will," along the way.

"I thank you," Laertes told them, "guard the door."

As the doors pulled together, Laertes advanced upon the King, his sword hardly swaying from its target. "Oh, you vile King ... *give me my father*!"

Gertrude rushed forward, moving in from Laertes' left – away from the sword itself – and pressed her hands against his chest. She slowed his march only slightly. "Calmly, good Laertes ..." she began.

"That drop of blood that's 'calm' proclaims me *bastard*," Laertes responded, his eyes never leaving the monarch, "cries betrayed husband to my father, and brands my true mother as the harlot – in this, of all places – between her chaste, unsmirched brows."

Still exhibiting an *unnerving* calm himself, Claudius asked, "What is the cause, Laertes, that your rebellion looks so giant-like?" He, too, stepped forward, until the three of them formed an intimate gathering near the center of the room. The tip of the young man's sword hovering bare inches from the Claudius' heart. "Let him go, Gertrude; do not fear for your husband and King – there's such divinity that hedge a King, that treason can have no more than a glance at what it would *like* to do, acts little of its will." Now the blade tip *was* touching him; he did not give the slightest flinch. "Tell me, Laertes ... why are you so incensed?" His eyes to one side. "Let him *go*, Gertrude." Then back to Laertes. "*Speak*, man."

Somewhat more in control of his tone, Laertes still demanded, "Where is my father?"

Claudius did not blink. "Dead."

Gertrude hurried to add, "But *not* by *him*."

The King gestured for her to be silent. "Let him demand his fill."

Laertes blinked back tears; the confirmation of the overwhelming rumor – which had impelled him to such rage – nearly broke him now. His sword arm finally began to waver, though it did not yet fall. "How *came* he dead? I'll not be juggled with – to *hell* with 'allegiance,' to the blackest *devil* with 'vows,' to the deepest *pit* with 'conscience' and 'grace' ... I - dare - *damnation*!" Again, the blade roused, once more the threat; Gertrude bit her lip, and held her tongue. "To this point I stand – I care not what the consequences are in this world or the next. Let come what comes; only I'll be *revenged* most thoroughly for my father."

Claudius arched an eyebrow. "Who shall stop you?"

"*My* will, not all the world's. And for my *means*, I'll join them so well, they shall go far with little."

Claudius nodded in visible consideration, then said softly, "Good Laertes ... if you desire to know the truth of your dear father's death ... is it written in your revenge, that, indiscriminately, you will draw both friend and foe, winner and loser ...?"

"None but his *enemies*."

"Will you *know* them, then?"

"I'll open my arms wide to his *good friends*; and, like the kind, life-rendering pelican mother, feed them with my blood."

Claudius smiled in approval. "Why, *now* you speak like a faithful son and a true gentleman. That I am *guiltless* of your father's death, and am most feelingly in *grief* for it ... it shall pierce your judgment as plainly as day does to eyes."

Laertes blinked stupidly, and finally broke his gaze away to seek council and confirmation from the Queen. Gertrude nodded in earnest – whatever crimes Claudius might have committed, he should certainly not pay for *this* one of which she, personally, knew for a fact that he was innocent.

Laertes clearly did not know what to do. Word had spread that, in some unknown way, the late Lord Chamberlain had somehow displeased the sovereign of Denmark – some even said that old Polonius suspected some involvement regarding the death of old King Hamlet? – and for that, Claudius had disposed of him. But now ... now...

The sword lowered an inch ... then two ...

"Let her come in!"

The voice of his roguish followers (even now, Laertes was feeling like a fool for having led such ragtag and bobtail into the palace) echoed through the room. The doors, which he had ordered closed, now opened.

Raging at the interruption to his most serious thoughts, Laertes turned and bellowed, "How now! What noise is that...?!"

And then his words dried up, the jaw hung slack, and his throat tightened at the sight of his sister, his dear, sweet Ophelia, staggering into the room with them, unkempt and looking like an escapee from some dark asylum, her arms no longer bound but still cloaked in the harness for that purpose.

Oh, heat, dry up my brains! Tears, seven times salt, burn out the feeling and powers of my eyes!

Ophelia – to the wedded couple's despair and Laertes' horror – had resumed her skipping around the perimeter. She had yet to sing (although Gertrude was merely grateful that she still abstained from her *screaming*), but she was indeed humming.

Laertes took one step toward her, then another. He reached out as though to touch her, despite the fact that the distance between them remained considerable.

"By Heaven," he spoke, "your madness shall be heavily paid for, till our scale turns the balance. Oh, rose of delicate May! Dear maid, kind sister, sweet Ophelia!"

Ophelia glanced his way, briefly, but did not halt her hop-skip stride. If there was recognition in her glance, it was minimal at best.

Oh, Heavens! Is it possible, a young maid's wits

should be as mortal as an old man's life? Nature is refined
in love, and where it is fine, it sends some precious proof of
itself after the thing it loves – her very love for her father
has caused her sanity to follow him into the grave!

Ophelia, meanwhile, had again taken up her song:
"They bore him barefaced on the bier;
Hey non nonny, nonny, hey nonny;
And in his grave rain'd many a tear: --
Fare you well, my dove!"

Now a tear ran down Laertes' cheek. He whispered,
"Had you your wits, and did you argue in favor of revenge,
it could not move thus."

Ophelia twirled, and twirled:
"You must sing a-down a-down,
An you call him a-down-a.
O, how the wheel becomes it! It is the false
steward, that stole his master's daughter."

Laertes' sword nearly slipped from his grasp as Ophelia
at last skipped toward him. "This nothing's more than lucid
speech."

His sister stopped before him, rocking as she fought for
balance against the sudden shift of momentum. She stared
up at him, smiled, then raised her hands to the side of her
head, her loose restraints trailing below her wrists like
streamers.

Laertes wanted to turn away, to avert his eyes, yet he
could not.

Ophelia twirled a respectable amount of her hair around
one finger, then yanked hard enough to rip it out at the roots.
Demonstrating no sign of discomfort, she freed the hair from
her finger, grasped it at the base with her other hand, and

presented the tomentum as though it were a bouquet.

"There's rosemary, that's for remembrance." She pressed the hair toward him; he felt compelled to accept it, which clearly pleased her. "Pray, love, remember." Another hand up, more torn hair, another offering. "And there is pansies, that's for thoughts."

Laertes took the second bundle with his own numb fingers. "A lesson contained in mad rambling, thoughts and remembrance fitted."

Ripping yet more hair, Ophelia skittered over to the King. "There's fennel for you, and columbines." Now she turned to the Queen. "There's rue for you. And here's some for me – we may call it herb-grace o' Sundays ..." She noticed that Gertrude was staring blankly at the offering, and instructed her kindly, "Oh, you must *wear* your rue with a difference. There's a daisy. I would give you some violets, but they all withered when my father died." Now she looked thoughtful. "They say he made a good end ..."

And then her hair-flowers seemed forgotten, and she was skipping once more:

"For bonny sweet Robin is all my joy ..."

Laertes watched her, helpless. "Melancholy and affliction, suffering, Hell itself ... she turns to charm and to prettiness."

"... And will he not come again?
And will he not come again?
No, no, he is dead:
Go to thy death-bed:
He never will come again.
His beard was as white as snow,
All flaxen was his poll:

He is gone, he is gone,
And we cast away moan:
God ha' mercy on his soul!"

Finally, her skipping took her back to the door by which she had entered. Indeed, a notable crack had formed down the center, as the Danes from without spied upon the spectacle – had he not felt so benumbed, Laertes might have been appalled.

"And of all Christian souls, I pray God!" Ophelia announced to them all and to no one. "God be with you!"

And then she was, once again, gone from sight.

Laertes' lips parted, and the barest sounds escaped, "... do you see this, oh, God ...?"

A sound behind him, then. A footstep, soft and cautious. He turned to find that Claudius had approached him, close enough to take his sword if that were his intention.

But instead, the King said, "Laertes ... I must consult with your grief, or you deny me fair treatment." He pointed toward the waiting mob. "Go but apart, make choice of whichever wisest friends you wish. And they shall hear and judge between you and me – if by direct or by indirect hand they find me guilty ... I will give my kingdom, my crown ... *my life* ... and all that I have, to you in *satisfaction*."

Now he drew closer still, his voice dropping. "But if *not* ... be content to lend your patience to me ... and we shall *jointly* labor with your soul to give it due content."

Laertes swallowed hard – his mouth was so dry that his tongue *clicked* audibly. "Let this be so," he agreed. "His manner of death, his obscure funeral – no marker, sword, nor memorial tablet over his bones, no noble rite nor formal ceremony – cry out to be heard, as if it were from Heaven to

Earth, that I *must* demand an explanation."

Claudius smiled, and while it was a smile of understanding, it was not exactly a smile of warmth. "So you shall ... and where the offence *is,* let the great axe *fall*."

Laertes met his gaze, and nodded his own understanding.

"I pray you," Claudius said, holding forth his arm in allegiance, "go with me."

Laertes went.

Horatio asked the servant, "Who are they that would speak with me?"

"Sailors, sir," the man answered as they strode through the corridor together. "They say they have *letters* for you."

Horatio nodded as they reached the crossway at the end. "Let them come in."

The servant bowed and disappeared around the corner. The entryway was only a short distance from where he waited ... but if these sailors bore the booty he *suspected* they might, then he did not want to greet them so openly.

I do not know from what part of the world I should be greeted, if not from Lord Hamlet.

A rustle of cloth and a clamor of booted footsteps were followed by the appearance of some rather artless and scraggly seamen. Forcing a welcoming grin to his lips, Horatio stepped forward to greet them as the servant gestured them into the corridor.

"God bless you, sir," the first sailor said with a thick accent.

"Let Him bless you, too," Horatio returned.

"He shall, sir, and may it please Him." He reached into an inner pocket of his grimy doublet and produced a crumpled envelope. "There's a letter for you, sir; it comes from the ambassador ..."

The "ambassador"? Horatio thought.

"... that was bound for England. If *your* name be

'Horatio,' as I am led to believe it is."

With something of a flourish, the sailor handed the envelope over. Horatio accepted it graciously, turned away from the men as they waited, and opened it with trembling fingers. In silence, he read ...

"Horatio,

When you have looked over this letter, give these fellows access to the King: They have letters for him.

Once we were two days old at sea, a pirate of very warlike equipment gave us chase. Finding ourselves too slow of sail, we put on a compelled fight, and in the grapple I boarded their ship. On that instant they got clear of our ship; so I, alone, became their prisoner. They have dealt with me like thieves of mercy, but they also knew what they did – I am to do a good turn for them.

Let the King have the letters I have sent; and you must come to me with as much speed as you would fly from death. I have words to speak to your ear that will leave you speechless; yet they are much too light for the size of the matter. These good fellows will bring you to where I am. Rosencrantz and Guildenstern still hold their course for England – of them, I have much to tell you.

Farewell.

He that you know to be yours,

Hamlet"

Returning the letter to its sheath, and then tucking the bundle into his vest, Horatio closed his eyes in long-anticipated relief.

Then he turned and addressed the patient sailors. "Come, I will make passage for your letters; and do it the *speedier*, that you may direct me to him from whom you brought them."

The first sailor smiled a gap-toothed smile and grunted his understanding.

PART FOUR
CHAPTER THREE

"Now your conscience must acknowledge my acquittal," said Claudius, "and you must put me in your heart as *friend*, since you have heard, and with a convinced ear, that he who slew your noble father pursued even *my* life."

The King of Denmark and his guest, Laertes, sat across from one another in the King's private chambers; not his office of state, not his personal rooms, but a discreet, obscure suite where ... *sensitive* business could safely be discussed.

As Laertes mulled over Claudius' proclamation, the King reached across and freshened the lad's drink. The younger man unmindfully reached out, took the goblet, and drank deeply.

"It appears well," Laertes admitted at last. "But tell me why you did not proceed against these wicked deeds – so criminal and punishable by death – as by your regard for your own safety, position, wisdom, all things else, you were powerfully stirred up."

"Oh, for two special reasons, which may to you, perhaps, seem much weak, but yet to me they are *strong* ...

"The Queen, his mother, lives almost by his looks; and for myself – my virtue or my plague, whichever it may be – she's so closely united to my life and soul, that, as the star could not move but in the sphere in which it is fixed ... *I* could not move except by *her*.

"The other motive – why I might not go to a public

reckoning – is the great love the *common people* bear him; who, dipping all his faults in their affection, would – like the spring that turns wood to stone – convert his shackles to graces. My arrows, too light for so loud a wind, would have returned to my bow again ... and *not* where I had aimed them."

Laertes nodded his bitter understanding. "And so *I* have lost a noble father; a sister driven into desperate circumstances, whose worth – if my praises may refer to as she was *before* this madness – stood as a pre-eminent challenger of all the age for her perfections ..." He gripped his goblet tighter. " ... *but my revenge will come.*"

"Do not break sleep for fear of losing *that*." Laertes glanced at Claudius, who offered an enigmatic smile in return. "You must not think that I am made of stuff so *spiritless* and *dull* that I can let my beard be shaken with danger and think it pastime. You shall hear more shortly." Now Claudius learned forward and said in earnest, "I loved your father, and I love myself; and that, I hope, will teach you to imagine—"

The door opened – the *primary* door; there were two others hidden in the walls – and a messenger appeared. Hoping against hope that the timing would be perfect, that he would receive news of Hamlet's fate in England, here, now, in front of Laertes, the King demanded, "How now! What news?"

The weedy young man stepped forward with a pair of documents. "Letters, my lord, from Hamlet: This to Your Majesty; this to the Queen."

A victorious smile started to creep its way across Claudius' features ... and then froze as the words registered.

"*From* ... from *Hamlet*?!" Surely he had misheard! "Who brought them?!"

The messenger fairly withered under his King's disapproval, but answered, "Sailors, my lord ... they *say* – I did not see them. They were given me by Claudio; he received them from the one who brought them."

Very nearly snarling, Claudius snatched both documents from the messenger's hand. "Laertes, you shall hear them." He snapped his fingers. "Leave us."

The messenger departed with haste and gratitude.

Opening the document addressed to himself, Claudius read aloud:

> "High and mighty,
> You shall know I am set destitute on your kingdom. Tomorrow I shall beg leave to see your kingly eyes; when I shall – first asking your permission to do so – recount the occasion of my sudden and most strange return.
>
>   HAMLET"

Claudius read the letter once more, this time silently, then – more of rhetoric than of Laertes – he asked, "What should this mean? Are *all* the rest coming back? Or is it some deceit, and no such thing?"

Laertes peered across at the paper. "Do you know the handwriting?"

Claudius nodded. "It is Hamlet's. 'Destitute.' And in a postscript here, he says 'alone.' " He pondered it a moment longer, than glanced at Laertes with a touch of glint in his eye. "Can you advise me?"

Laertes' face simultaneously brightened and darkened. "I'm lost in it, my lord ... but *let* him come; it warms the very sickness in my heart, that I shall live and tell him to his teeth, 'Thus you die.' "

"If it is to be so, Laertes – how can he have returned? Yet, clearly he has – will you be ruled by me?"

A heartbeat passed. Then, "Aye, my lord; provided that you will not overrule me to a peace."

"To your *own* peace. If he has now returned, turning from his voyage that he means to undertake no more ... I will work him to an exploit, now ripe in my mind, under that which he shall not choose but fall. And for his *death*, no wind of blame shall breathe, but even his mother shall exonerate the incident ... and call it an *accident*."

In insalubrious exhilaration, Laertes rushed to say, "My lord, I will be ruled; if you could devise it so that *I* might be the instrument."

"It happens right," Claudius agreed with a casual wave of his hand. "You have been talked of much since your travel – and within Hamlet's hearing – for a skill wherein, they say, you shine. Your other accomplishments put together did not pluck such *envy* from him as did that *one* ... and that, in my regard, of the least importance."

"What skill is *that*, my lord ...?"

But Claudius offered another enigmatic smile. "A very ribbon in the cap of youth, yet needful too – for *youth* becomes the light and careless garb that it wears no less than settled *age* becomes his prosperous and dignified sables and his garments." Casually, almost seeming to Laertes as though he were changing the subject, he went on, "Two months ago, a gentleman visited here from Normandy: I've seen and served against the French, and they are skilled on horseback ... but *this* gallant gentleman had *witchcraft* in it; he grew unto his seat; and to such wondrous doing brought his horse, as if he had been made one body and combined the brave beast. So far he surpassed my thought, that I – in mere imagining of shapes and tricks – come short of what he did."

"A Norman, was it?"

"A Norman."

Then Laertes' eyes widened. "Upon my life ... *Lamond*?"

Claudius grinned. "The very same."

"I know him well: He is indeed the ornament and gem of all the nation."

"He testified to your excellence, and gave you such a masterly report for your exercise in the art of *self-defense*, and for your *rapier* most especially, that he cried out, 'it would be a sight indeed' if anyone could match you – the fencers of their nation, he swore, had neither motion, guard, nor eye, if you opposed them." Then Claudius stressed, "Sir, Hamlet did so envenom this report with his *envy* that he could nothing do but wish and beg your speedy return, to fence with you. Now, out of this ..." But then Claudius fell silent as he contemplated the young man further.

It was, of course, a carefully calculated pause.

"*What* out of this, my lord?" Laertes demanded with agitation and petulance.

"Laertes ... was your father *dear* to you? Or are you like the *painting* of sorrow, a face without a heart?"

Aghast, Laertes spat, "*Why* do you ask this?"

"Not that I think you did not love your father," Claudius

replied with placation, "but that I know love is begun by *circumstance*; and that I see, by the test of experience, circumstance qualifies the spark and fire of it. But, to the *quick* of the ulcer: Hamlet ... comes ... back. *What* would you undertake, to show yourself your father's son in deed more than in words?"

Laertes considered the question for the briefest moment, his eyes gazing forward but seeing not this room, nor the here and now. When he spoke, his voice was a hateful whisper. "I would cut his throat in the church."

Claudius approved of this response. "Indeed, no place should offer asylum to *murder*; and *revenge* should have no bounds. But, good Laertes, if you will *do* this, keep close within your chamber. Hamlet, once returned, shall know you have come home – we'll incite those who shall praise your excellence and set a double varnish on the fame the Frenchman already gave you. Finally, we'll bring you together and wager on your heads. He – being easy-going, magnanimous, and innocent – will not think to inspect the foils; so that with ease, or with a little cunning, you may choose an unblunted sword, and in a tricky thrust ... repay him for your father."

Warming to the plot, Laertes further suggested, "I will do it. *And*, for that purpose, I'll *anoint* my sword." When the King raised an eyebrow in question, he explained, "I bought an ointment from a traveling 'doctor' that is *so* deadly that, if you but dip a knife in it, wherever it draws blood ... *no* plaster so rare, collected from *all* medicinal herbs that have curative power under the moon, can save the thing from death that is but *scratched* with it. I'll score my point with this contagion so that, if I graze him even slightly, it will mean *death*."

Claudius was pleased. "Let's further think of this; weigh what convenience both of time and means may best suit our needs. If this should *fail*, and then our purpose shines through our bad performance, it would be better not assayed – therefore, this project *should* have a back-up plan that might hold, *if* this should burst when tested." Reining himself in, he warned both Laertes and himself, "Soft! Now ... let me see ... we'll make a solemn wager on your skills ..." He snapped his fingers. "I have it! When in your exertion you are hot and dry – and you should make your bouts more violent to that end – and when he calls for drink, I'll have prepared him a chalice for the occasion ... whereon by sipping – if he, by chance, escapes your venomed strike – our purpose may hold *there*." A sound echoed through the office, and both men jumped like the scheming parties they knew themselves to be. "But stay, what noise ...?"

A moment later, Gertrude entered the room.

"How now, sweet Queen!" Claudius called, reaching out for her, his smile just as "sweet" as his words ... but upon a second look, the King realized that his efforts to cover his tracks were unnecessary.

Gertrude looked awful. Her hands were wringing, her cheeks were sallow, and her eyes were wet and reddened. She shuffled toward them with a shaky and uncertain gait. Claudius was on the verge of asking what in the world had happened when at last she spoke, her eyes downcast.

"One woe does tread upon another's heel ..." she whispered in a broken voice, "... so fast they follow ..." Now she forced her gaze upward, and locked eyes with the younger man. Drawing a breath, she announced, "Your sister ... has ... *drowned*, Laertes."

Silence. Then, "Drowned. Oh ... where?"

Shock, Claudius noted. *It is shock.* He turned away.

Gertrude went on, with observable effort, "There is a willow that grows sideways over a brook, that shows its grey-white leaves in the glassy stream.   There, with willow   branches,   she   made   fantastic   garlands   of buttercups, nettles, daisies, and the early purples that free-spoken shepherds give a grosser name, but our chaste maids call 'dead men's fingers' ... there, she clambered to hang her garlanded weeds on the pendent boughs ... and the envious sliver *broke*. She and her weedy trophies fell down into the weeping brook. Her clothes spread wide; and, mermaid-like, for a while, they bore her up ... at which time, she chanted snatches of old hymns, as one unaware of her own distress, or like a creature native and habituated unto that element. But ... it was not long until her garments, heavy with their drink, pulled the poor wretch from her melodious lay ... to muddy death."

"Alas, then ... she is drowned?"

"Drowned," the Queen nodded, "drowned."

Scarcely above a whisper, no longer looking to the Queen but again to the floor, Laertes said, "*Too much* of water you have, poor Ophelia ... and therefore I *forbid* my tears. But yet, weeping is our natural way; nature holds to her customs, let shame say what it will: When these *tears* are gone, my feminine traits will be gone." He glanced sideways at Claudius. "Adieu, my lord – I have a speech of fire, that willingly would blaze ... but that this folly drowns it."   Skirting   around   the   Queen,   mumbling something of an apology to her as well, he shuffled dumbly from the room.

Sighing, Claudius said, "Let's follow him, Gertrude – how much I had to do to calm his rage! Now I fear this will start it again; therefore ..." He reached for her hand. "... let's follow."

PART FIVE
CHAPTER ONE

Most men can endure the cold. If they must, if the need arises. They might not *enjoy* it, but they can bear it.

Likewise, most men can stand the darkness of night; the ghostly touch of a fog; the sounds of the nocturnal creatures, those Will-o'-the-Wisp-styled fauna that make the moon their sun. All of these things, most men can abide.

Notably *fewer* men, however, can stand the occupation of an old graveyard ... in the cold, in the dark, within the fog, surrounded by the sounds of unseen beasts around them.

Fewer men indeed.

Some men, however, have the misfortune of vocations that *require* all of these ingredients. If they are to survive (and keep their sanity), they must be made of sterner stuff ... *or* possess a wondrous sense of humor.

Looking around the churchyard cemetery, resting his spade even as his partner made use of his own, the first rustic inquired of the second, "Is she to be buried in *Christian* burial, when she willfully seeks her own salvation?"

The second rustic shrugged. "I tell you she is – and therefore we make her grave at once. The coroner has passed judgment on her, and finds it 'Christian burial.' "

But the first was not satisfied. "How can that be ... unless she drowned herself in her own defense?"

Unimpressed with his partner's attempt at wry humor, the second grunted and replied, "Why, it is found so."

The first grunted his own dismissal. "It *must* be 'in self-defense;' it cannot be else. For here lies the point: If I drown myself wittingly, it argues an act. And an act has three branches ..." He counted off on his fingers. "It is to *act*, to *do*, and to *perform*. Ergo, she drowned herself wittingly."

The second shook his head. "Nay, but hear you, Mr. Sexton—"

"Give me leave." His hands pantomimed along. "Here lies the water, good; here stands the man, good. If the man goes to this water, and drowns himself, it is – will he, will he not – he goes. Mark you that. But if the water comes to him and drowns him, he drowns *not* himself. Ergo, he that is *not* guilty of his own death shortens not his own *life*."

"But is this law?"

The first rustic shrugged. "Aye, marry, is it; coroner's inquest law."

"Will you have the truth on it?" He dug his spade deep into the earth. "If this had not been a gentlewoman, she would have been buried *out* of Christian burial."

A chuckle. "Why, there you say it. And the more pity that great folk should have countenance in this world to drown or hang themselves, more than their fellow Christians." With a parody of grace, his took up his tool at last. "Come, my spade. There is no ancient gentleman but gardeners, ditchers, and grave-makers: They sustain Adam's profession."

The second scratched his head in confusion. "Was *he* a gentleman?"

The first waggled his finger knowingly. "He was the first that ever bore arms."

"Why, he *had* no coat of arms."

Mock dismay from the first. "What, are you a *heathen*?

How do you understand the Scripture? The Scripture says, 'Adam digged.' Could he *dig* without arms? I'll put another question to you: If you answer me not to the purpose, confess yourself a fool—"

"Out with it," the second grumbled with impatience.

"What is he that builds stronger than either the mason, the shipwright, or the carpenter?"

The second considered this for a moment. "The gallows-maker; for *that* frame outlives a thousand tenants."

The first laughed aloud. "I like your wit well, in good faith. The gallows does well ... but *how* does it well? It does well to those that do in – now you do *ill* to say the gallows is built stronger than the church. Ergo, the gallows may do well to *you*. Try it again, come now."

" 'Who builds stronger than a mason, a shipwright, or a carpenter?' "

"Aye. Tell me that, and you can call it a day!"

"Marry, *now* I can tell you."

A smirk. "Get to it."

The second thought hard. Harder still. Then he spat on the ground and seized up his spade in frustration. "By the mass, I cannot tell."

As the rustics prattled on, they failed to notice that they were no longer quite alone. They had developed such thick skins against being "jumpy" here in the graveyard, they had actually dulled themselves to the point where they did not attend the presence of company – *living* company.

"Cudgel your brains about it no more," said the first to the second, "for your dull ass will not mend his pace with beating; and, when you are next asked this question, answer 'a grave-maker' – the houses that *he* makes last till doomsday." Taking up his spade with a flamboyant twirl, he shooed his partner away. "Go, get you to Yaughan: Fetch me a stoup of liquor!"

The second rustic grumbled his displeasure, tossed down his tool, and stomped off into the fog ... still not seeing the pair of figures who slowly made their way toward the grave that was the rustics' unfinished task.

Digging into the ground as he swayed to his own melody, the first rustic sang:

"In youth, when I did love, did love,
Methought it was very sweet,
To contract, O, the time, for, ah, my behove,
O, methought, there was nothing meet."

He danced and careened and dug, and still paid no attention to his spontaneous audience ...

Watching from the shadows, Prince Hamlet asked of Horatio, "Has this fellow no feeling of his business, that he *sings* at grave-making?"

Horatio shrugged. "Habit has made property of *easiness* in him." He gestured around the old cemetery and shrugged again.

Hamlet nodded, conceding the point. "It is even so: The hand of little employment has the more delicate sense."

And the rustic sang on:

"But age, with his stealing steps,
Hath claw'd me in his clutch,
And hath shipped me intil the land,
As if I had never been such."

Upon his next shovelful of earth, an aged, decayed, human skull broke loose and flew from its grave onto the growing pile of soil ... and the rustic thought absolutely nothing of it.

Hamlet shook his head in mild disdain. "That skull had a tongue in it, and could sing once – how the knave dashes it to the ground, as if it were the jawbone of Cain, he who committed the first murder! It might be the skull of a schemer, which this ass now gets the better of; one that would bypass God's laws, might it not?"

Horatio shrugged a third time. "It might, my lord." He was clearly uninterested in the happenstance of their surroundings, and more intent to get back to the matters at hand.

But Hamlet was not easily dissuaded. "Or of a courtier, which could say, 'Good morrow, sweet lord! How are you, good lord?' This might be my lord such-a-one, that praised my lord such-a-one's horse, when he meant to beg it, might it not?"

"Aye, my lord."

"Why, even so ... and now my Lady Worm's; its lower jaw gone, and knocked about the head with a sexton's spade. *Here's* fine revolution, and we had the trick to see it. Did these bones cost no more the breeding, but to play a game of loggats with them? *Mine* ache to think on it."

The rustic continued digging, and singing:

"A pick-axe, and a spade, a spade,
for and a shrouding sheet:
O, a pit of clay for to be made
For such a guest is meet."

His tool struck another point of resistance, he pried, and up came another decrepit skull. He tossed this one aside, too.

"There's another," Hamlet commented as he and

Horatio drew steadily closer to the action. "Why, may not that be the skull of a lawyer? Where be his subtleties now, his fine distinctions, his cases, his land titles, and his tricks? Why does he now allow this rude knave to knock him about the head with a dirty shovel, and will not tell him of his action of battery?" He scoffed. "Hum! This fellow might be in his time a great buyer of land, with his statutes, his bonds, his fines, his double vouchers, his recoveries. Is *this* the fine of his fines, and the recovery of his recoveries, to have his fine skull full of fine dirt? Will his vouchers vouch him no more of his purchases, and double ones, too, than the length and breadth of a pair of legal documents? The very transfers of his lands will hardly lie in the skull itself; and must the *owner* himself have no more, ha?"

"Not a jot more, my lord."

"Is not parchment made of sheepskins?"

"Aye, my lord, and of calf-skins, too."

"They are sheep and calves, which seek out assurance in that. I will speak to this fellow." Horatio reached forward, to take his Prince's arm and advise against it. But it was too late; Hamlet was already treading forward and calling out, "Whose grave's this, little sir?"

The rustic was startled only slightly, his thick skin against fright ever evident. "*Mine*, sir," he quipped, and went right on singing:

"O, a pit of clay for to be made
For such a guest is meet."

Hamlet smiled. "I think it is yours, indeed; for *you* lie in it."

The rustic glanced briefly about himself – he was now chest-deep in the earth – but thought nothing of it. He returned, "You lie out of it, sir, and therefore it is not yours. For my part, I do not *lie* in it ... and yet it is mine."

Hamlet's smile grew; he enjoyed this knave's wit. "You *do* lie in it; to be in it and say it is yours – it is for the dead, not for the quick; therefore ... you *lie*."

Now the rustic was smiling, too. "It is a quick lie, sir; it will away again, from me to you."

"What man do you dig it for?"

"For no man, sir."

Hamlet chuckled. "What *woman*, then?"

"For none, neither."

"*Who* is to be buried in it?"

"One that *was* a woman, sir; but, rest her soul, she's dead."

Hamlet laughed now, and – seeking shared appreciation – turned to Horatio. The rustic, for his part, returned to his work. "How *absolute* the knave is! We must speak meticulously, or ambiguity will undo us. By the Lord, Horatio, for three years I have taken note of it: The age is grown so *refined* that the toe of the peasant comes so near the foot of the courtier, he rubs the courtier's chaffed heel." He again addressed the rustic, "How long have you been a grave-maker?"

"Of all the days in the year, I came to it that same day that our last king, Hamlet, overcame Old Fortinbras."

"How long ago was that?"

The rustic rolled his eyes theatrically. "You cannot tell *that*? Every fool can tell *that*: It was the very day that young Hamlet was born ... he who is mad, and was sent to England."

Hamlet nodded, amused. "Aye, marry ... why *was* he

sent to England?"

Now the rustic answered as though he were speaking to a small child. He tapped his own temple, then twirled his finger around in a slow circle. "Why ... *because - he - was - mad*." He then gestured it away. "He shall recover his wits there; or, if he does not, it's no great matter there."

"Why?"

"It will not be *seen* in him there; there the men are as *mad* as he."

Again, Hamlet nodded. Behind him, Horatio shuffled. "How did he come to be 'mad?' "

"Very strangely, they say."

"*How* strangely?"

"He lost his wits."

"Upon what grounds?"

The rustic smirked. "Why, *here* in Denmark!" Hamlet groaned and chuckled at the pun. And then the rustic finally answered the original question. "I have been sexton here, man and boy, for thirty years."

Hamlet glanced down at the skulls upon the pile of dirt. "How long will a man lie in the earth before he rots?"

"In faith, if he is not rotten *before* he die – and we have many disease-rotten corpses nowadays, that will scarcely endure the laying in the ground – he will last for some eight or nine years. A *tanner* will definitely last nine years."

"Why he more than another?"

"Why, sir, his hide is so *tanned* with his trade, that he will keep out water a great while; and water is a grievous decayer of a diseased, dead body." He looked down into the grave, and for a moment he poked with his spade, prodded with his foot. Finally, he stooped down from sight, then arose bearing yet another human artifact. "*Here's* a skull now; this skull has lain in the earth for three and twenty years."

Intrigued, Hamlet asked, "Whose was it?"

"A plagued, mad fellow's, it was – whose do *you* think it was?"

"No, I do not know."

"A pestilence on him for a mad rogue! He poured a flagon of Rhenish on my head once." He held the domed item aloft for showcase. "*This* same skull, sir, was *Yorick's* skull, the King's jester."

Until now, Hamlet had engaged the man with idle interest – as his friend Horatio suspected, he participated as an act of escapism, to perhaps bide some time away from the mortal troubles that had overwhelmed his life.

But *now* the rustic held the Prince's full attention. He eyed the rotten, surprisingly small skull with keen interest.

"*This*?" he asked.

The rustic smiled. "Even that."

"Let me see."

The rustic handed it over with indifference, then listened on with only half-an-ear as he returned once again to his work.

Hamlet held the skull gingerly upon his fingertips. "Alas, poor Yorick! I knew him, Horatio: A fellow of infinite jest, of most excellent fancy! He has borne me on his back a thousand times; and now ... how abhorred in my imagination it is! My gorge rises at it." He pointed with his other hand. "*Here* hung those lips that I have kissed I do not know how often." He spoke to the skull, "Where be your gibes now? Your gambols? Your songs? Your flashes of merriment, that so easily set the table on a roar?" He shook his head. "Not one now, to mock your own grinning? Quite down in the mouth?" He craned his neck forward, and lowered his voice as though to whisper into the dead man's nonexistent ear. "Now, get you to my lady's chamber, and tell her, let her paint an inch thick, to this appearance she must come – make her laugh at that."

After a moment of silence, Hamlet lowered the skull – though he did not release it – and turned to his friend. "Prithee, Horatio, tell me one thing."

"What's that, my lord?"

"Do you think Alexander the Great looked of this fashion in the earth?"

"Even so," Horatio mused.

Hamlet sniffed, then made a face and added, "And smelt so? Pah!" With some distaste, but plenty of respect, he lowered the skull to the ground, placing it not on top of the dirt pile, but next to it.

Horatio offered a lopsided grin. "Even so, my lord."

"To what base uses we may return, Horatio! Why, may not imagination trace the noble dust of Alexander, till he finds it stopping a bunghole?"

"It would be to consider too *closely*, to consider so."

"No, faith, not a jot; but to follow him thusly with moderation enough, and likelihood to lead it. As thus: Alexander died, Alexander was buried, Alexander returned into dust; the dust is earth; of earth we make loam; and why of that loam, to where he was converted ... might they not stop a beer-barrel?"

And suddenly he whispered a soft sing-song:

"Imperious Caesar, dead and turn'd to clay,

Might stop a hole to keep the wind away:
O, that that earth, which kept the world in
   awe,
Should patch a wall to expel the winter flaw!"

Perhaps he would have continued further, perhaps not ... regardless, he was interrupted by the appearance of a torch-lit funeral party, making their way toward this very grave site. A single bell rang with every other collective step, and he was surprised that he had not heard them before. At first, he merely regarded them with the same caution he would have afforded any group of strangers at this late hour ... but then his eyes widened.

"But soft! But soft!" He gestured to Horatio. "Come aside: Here comes the *King*."

Dragging Horatio with him, he faded back into the mist and trees. The rustic watched their sudden retreat with a raised eyebrow ... then dismissed the matter, and hurried to complete his own work.

As best Hamlet could make out through the fog and shadows, the morose party consisted of Claudius and Gertrude (he was pleased to see that his mother was *not* holding the villain's hand, as she surely would have been before he was shipped from Denmark), a Priest and his attendants, some dozen courtiers – who also bore the coffin upon their shoulders – and another young man, whose head was down and so Hamlet could not clearly see his face.

"The Queen, the courtiers," he whispered, "but whom is this funeral for? And with such lack of customary ceremony, here in the dead of night? This suggests the corpse they follow did, with a desperate hand, forsake its own life ... but it was of some notable *rank*. We'll conceal ourselves here awhile, and watch."

The party came to a halt next to the fresh grave; the rustic scrambled to clear the way, tossing one final set of skull and shoulder bones onto the dirt pile as he scampered to one side. The man whom Hamlet had failed to recognize lifted his head and removed his hat. "What other ceremony will there be ...?" the familiar young man asked the priest.

Hamlet leaned closer to Horatio's ear. "That is *Laertes*, a very noble youth – listen carefully."

In the meantime, Laertes had been displeased with the priest's failure to answer, and he repeated in a harsher voice, "What other *ceremony* will there *be?*"

Appearing quite uncomfortable, the priest glanced at the King, then replied, "Her obsequies have been extended as far as we have sanction. Her death was ... *doubtful* ..." His eyes again flickered toward Claudius. "... and if not for that great command overruling the customary procedures ... she would certainly have been lodged, unsanctified, in the ground until the final trumpet blast of the Archangel. Instead of charitable prayers, shards, flints, and pebbles would have been thrown upon her body ... and yet, here she *is*, allowed her virgin garland, her unmarried flowers upon the grave, and her burial in consecrated earth, with the church bell tolling."

The man's *distaste* was evident, but Laertes still pleaded, "Must there be *nothing more* done?"

"*Nothing more* done," the priest insisted. "We would profane the service of the dead to sing a dirge and such rest to her as to piously-deceased souls."

With sad acceptance and a dose of anger, Laertes conceded. "Lay her in the earth." The courtiers obeyed, settled their burden into the hole the rustics had so recently completed. And as the deed commenced, Laertes faced the priest and spat, "And from her fair and unpolluted flesh may *violets* spring forth! I tell you, graceless priest ... *my sister* shall be a ministering angel when *you* lie howling among the damned in *Hell*."

Hamlet gasped. Did Laertes say his ... *sister*?! Feeling dizzy, he gripped Horatio's shoulder and choked, "What, the fair Ophelia!"

The Queen began tossing blooms into the grave upon the coffin. "Flowers to the sweet," she called, "farewell! I had hoped you would have been my Hamlet's wife; I thought to have decorated your bride-bed, sweet maid, and not have strewed your grave."

Laertes was crying now. "Oh, treble woe ... fall *ten times* treble on that cursed head, whose wicked deed deprived you of your most common sense!" Then the first shovelful of dirt struck the top of Ophelia's coffin ... and Laertes broke. "Hold off the earth awhile," he screamed, "until I have held her once more in my arms!"

And with that, to the horror of everyone present – including the two observers in the dark – Laertes leaped down into the grave. He pried at the lid of the coffin and, with some effort, the hastily-constructed wooden casket gave way. Laertes pulled the stiffened remains of his sister to his chest and cried, "*Now* pile your dust upon the quick and dead, until you have made a mountain of this ground, to overtop old Mount Pelion, or the skyish head of blue Mount Olympus!"

Finally, Hamlet could bite his tongue no more. Trembling, he emerged from his hiding place to the shock of all, but it was to Laertes he looked as he said, "What is he whose grief bears such an inflated emphasis? Whose phrase of sorrow casts a spell upon all the planets, and makes them stand like wonder-wounded hearers? This is *I*, Hamlet, the true King of Denmark!"

And with that, he, too, leaped into the grave.

While everyone else remained stunned, Laertes did not hesitate. "The Devil take your soul!" He threw himself at Hamlet, his hands seeking the Prince's throat.

Even as they struggled, Hamlet rasped, "You do not pray well. I ask you, take your fingers from my throat ... for, though I am not quick-tempered and rash ... I have something *dangerous* in me yet ... which your *wisdom* should know to *fear*. Remove your hands!"

In spite of the perverse pleasure it gave Claudius to see Hamlet in such a state, the King knew this was neither the proper time nor circumstance. He snapped at the rooted courtiers, "Pluck them asunder!"

It was as though his commanding voice had broken a choke-hold, not on Hamlet, but on everyone else present. The courtiers rushed forward; Gertrude cried, "Hamlet, Hamlet!"; there were calls of "Gentlemen!" Bodies rushed to and fro, and the men were separated and pulled from the grave. Claudius placed a hand upon Laertes' shoulder, as Horatio made a similar gesture with Hamlet.

"Please, my lord," Horatio pleaded, "be still."

His breath gushing, Hamlet said, "Why, I will fight with him upon this theme until my eyelids will no longer wag!"

"Oh, my son," Gertrude wept, "*what* theme?"

What theme, indeed. Dare he say it? He, who treated this dear, sweet, lovely girl with such disdain before he left?

He, who decided in a heartbeat that she had betrayed him, yet did not give her the slightest opportunity to suggest her innocence? Surely he was not such a *hypocrite* ...?

And yet, before the sight of his cold, dead dearest, he could not help but answer, "*I loved Ophelia*! Forty thousand brothers, with all their quantity of love, could not make up *my* sum! What will *you* do for her?"

The insult was almost enough to send Laertes forward once more, but Claudius held him fast, sneering, "Oh, he is *mad*, Laertes."

Even Gertrude touched Laertes' arm. "For the love of God," she begged, "leave him alone!"

Now Hamlet was crying as well, and he still demanded of Laertes, "Christ's wounds, show me what you will *do* for her! Will you weep?! Will you fight?! Will you fast? Will you tear yourself? Will you drink up vinegar? Eat a crocodile? *I will do it*. Did you come here to *whine*? To *outface* me with leaping in her grave? Be buried quick with her, and so will *I*. And if you talk of 'mountains,' let them throw *millions* of acres upon us, till our ground – singeing its scalp against the sphere of the sun – makes Mount Ossa like a wart! No, and if you will mouth on, I'll rant as well as you!"

For the moment, Laertes refrained from rising to the bait. The Queen took his face in her hands, turning him away from her son to see only her. "This is utter *madness*," she insisted, "and thus, in a while, the fit will work itself out of him; anon, as calm as the female dove, when her golden babes are hatched, his silence will sit drooping."

Indeed, Hamlet was already calming, his torrent of pain having drained him. He slumped against Horatio, but still he asked of Laertes, albeit in a cooler voice, "Hear me, sir ... what is the reason that you use me thus? I have always loved *you*, too ..." He shook his head. "... but it is no matter. Let Hercules himself do what he may, the cat will mew and dog will have his day."

With that, Hamlet pulled free of the hands around him, and stumbled off into the mist from which he had emerged, his feet shuffling and his head hanging.

Even as he faded from sight, Claudius said in a low voice, "I pray you, good Horatio, wait upon him."

Horatio nodded out of forced respect and hurried to catch his friend.

Claudius now turned to the still-quaking Laertes. He continued in an even lower voice, "Strengthen your patience in recalling our last night's speech; we'll put the matter to the immediate test ..."

It was then that Claudius realized that Gertrude was watching him – watching him with a suspicious eye. How dare she?! Was her son's latest display *still* not enough to demonstrate—

But alas, it mattered not. For now, he required *privacy*.

"Good Gertrude," he said as reasonably as he might, "set some watch over your son."

Gertrude continued staring at him a moment longer; if anything, her mistrustful gaze grew more fierce ... but then she nodded, and gestured for some courtiers to accompany her as she, too, followed after Hamlet.

When she was a good distance away, Claudius returned his attention to Laertes. "This grave," he promised, "shall have an enduring monument – an hour of quiet shortly shall we see ... until then, in *patience* our proceeding be."

Laertes met his eye ... and a small smile grew upon his lips. A knowing smile they shared together.

Hamlet thrust open the double doors to his personal chambers and looked around. How long had it been since he had been *happy* within these walls ...?

As Horatio joined him, he produced a weathered, rumpled set of documents and handed them over to his friend. "So much for this, sir – *now* you shall hear the other news I have to share with you. You *do* remember all the circumstances?"

Taking the letters, Horatio asked with some indignation, "*Remember* it, my lord?"

"Sir, in my heart there was a kind of fighting, that would not let me sleep – I thought I lay worse than the mutineers in the heavy shackles. On impulse – and praised be 'impulse' for it – let us acknowledge that our indiscretion sometimes serves us well, when our deep plots come to nothing. And that should teach us that there's a *divinity* that shapes our ends, however we first *block* that divinity—"

"*That* is most certain."

Hamlet nodded, pleased that his friend understood his meaning. At last, he drew a deep breath, and told Horatio of the events that brought him back to this place.

"Up from my cabin, my sea-gown wrapped about me, in the dark ... I groped to find Rosencrantz and Guildenstern; I *had* my desire. I stole their packet, and finally withdrew back to my own room again. I was so bold, my fears forgetting manners, to unseal their commission papers ...

where I *found*, Horatio – oh, royal knavery! – an *exact command*, garnished with many different sorts of reasons concerning Denmark's health and England's, too, with – ho, such bugs and goblins in my life! – that, upon the perusal, no time lost, no, not even to wait for the sharpening of the axe ... my head should be *chopped off.*"

Hamlet had reached his couch, and as he turned to sit, he discovered that Horatio had frozen in his tracks upon hearing this last proclamation. "Is it *possible*?" Horatio asked, barely louder than a whisper.

With a weary sigh, Hamlet seated himself, pointing at the documents in Horatio's hands as he did so. "*There's* the commission: Read it at your leisure. But will you listen to how I did proceed?"

"I beseech you."

"Being thus ensnared round with villains – before I could make a prologue to my brain, it had begun its play ... I sat me down, devised a *new* commission, wrote it beautifully." He chuckled without any real humor. "I did once possess, as our statesmen do, a 'lowly talent' to write with such attractive skill, and I had labored to *forget* that learning ... but, sir, *now* it did me good and faithful service. Would you like to know the gist of what I wrote?"

Horatio, now sitting himself across the couch from his Prince, answered, "Aye, good my lord."

The Prince smiled, and now a trace of humor *was* visible to Horatio – and *dark* humor it was, indeed. "An earnest conjuration from our King," he said, dripping sarcasm between his words, "as *England* was his faithful tributary, as *love* between them like a palm might flourish, as *peace* should always wear her wheaten garland and stand as connection between their friendship – and many such 'As'es like great *asses* – upon the view and knowing of these contents, without further debate, without the slightest deviation from these orders ... the King of England should put the *bearers* of these orders to sudden *death*, with no time for absolution allowed."

Horatio was aghast at the eternal implications therein. But, trying to keep his expression sympathetic – or at least *neutral* – he asked, "How ... how was this sealed?"

"Why, even in *that,* Heaven was guiding. I had my father's *signet* in my purse, which was an exact likeness of the Danish seal! I folded the writ up in the same form as the original, signed it, gave it the royal impression, and replaced it safely ... the substitute never recognized." He held his cold smile through a moment of reflection, then made a casual, dismissing gesture. "Now, the next day was our sea-fight; and what followed that you already know."

Horatio remained silent for a moment. At last, he was unable to keep from observing, "So ... Guildenstern and Rosencrantz are going to their deaths."

Hamlet shrugged. "Why, man, they did *make love* to this employment; they are not near my conscience. Their ruin grows from their own interference: It is dangerous when the *inferior* come between the thrust and fierce points of mighty opponents."

Horatio was still uneasy with his friend's callous disregard for their former classmates ... but he had to admit that it was not *Hamlet* who prompted these hostilities. "Why, what a *King* is this!"

"Does it not, you think, stand as an *obligation* to me now – he that has killed my King and father, and whored my mother, popped in between the election as King of Denmark and my hopes, thrown out his hook and line for my very life, and with such trickery – is it not perfect conscience, to repay him with this arm? And is it not to be *damned*, to let this cancerous sore of our nature grow into yet *further* evil?"

Before he could answer, another thought occurred to Horatio. "It must be shortly known to him from England what is the issue of the business there!"

"It *will* be short – the interim is *mine*. And to take a man's life takes no more time than to say, 'One.' But I am very sorry, good Horatio, that I ... forgot myself with Laertes. For, by the image of *my* cause, I see the portrait of *his*. I'll court his favor – but, to be sure, the pretentious expression of his grief did put me into a towering passion."

Before Horatio could make whatever reply he might have offered, the chamber door rattled. He stood, stepping slightly in front of his Prince, this latest revelation of the King's villainy having unnerved him. "Peace! Who comes here?"

The door – at long last, and after what seemed an odd amount of difficulty – opened, admitting a young, overdressed courtier. The man snapped to attention, removed his rather elaborate chapeau from his head and tucking it under his arm.

Hamlet rose unenthusiastically to his feet. *Osric.*

"Your lordship is right welcome back to Denmark," young Osric smarmed.

"I humbly thank you, sir." He turned slightly toward Horatio (though not all the way) and lowered his voice (though not a great deal) as he asked, "Do you know this water-fly...?"

Horatio shrugged. "No, my good lord."

"Your state is the more virtuous; for it is a *vice* to know him. He has much land, and fertile, too – if a *beast* were named lord of other *beasts*, it would find itself standing in the King's court: He is a small, chattering jackdaw ... but, as I said, a bird spacious in the possession of dirt."

Uncertain as to how to react to the words, which Hamlet had intended him to at least *partially* overhear, Osric snapped to attention yet again and announced, "Sweet lord, if your lordship were at leisure, I should impart something to you from his majesty."

"I will receive it, sir, with all attentiveness of spirit." Then Hamlet offered a vague gesture toward the man's flamboyant hat. "Put your bonnet to its proper use; it is for the head."

Taken off-guard, Osric glance down at his hat as though he had never seen it before. A moment later, he replied with an uncertain, "I ... thank your lordship ... but it is very hot."

"No, believe me, it is very cold; the wind is northerly."

Horatio had to smother a grin as poor Osric – never one to argue with royalty – maneuvered his hat back up onto his head. "It *is* somewhat cold, my lord, indeed."

Hamlet cocked his head to one side, as though he were a painter evaluating his latest work. His expression grew disapproving, and he now said, "And yet, I think it *is* very sultry and hot for my mood."

"Exceedingly, my lord; it is *very* sultry ..." Down again came the hat. "... as it were, I cannot tell how." And now, back to business. "But, my lord, his majesty bade me signify to you that he has laid a great *wager* upon your head: Sir, this is the matter—"

But, poor Osric, Hamlet was not quite finished having fun with him. He gestured for Osric to once again return the hat to his head, as though he'd never rescinded his comment about the cold. "I beseech you, remember ..."

Horatio could barely contain his amusement now.

Osric considered his hat once more, and it finally dawned upon him that the Prince was finding pleasure at his expense. Swallowing audibly, he decided to risk regal disfavor and take a stand for himself.

"No, my good lord ... for my *ease*, in good faith ...?"

Smirking, Hamlet gave up the game and indicated that Osric should continue his assignment.

"Sir, Laertes has newly returned to court. Believe me, he is an absolute *gentleman*, full of most excellent qualities, of very gentle society and splendid appearance – indeed, to speak feelingly of him, he is the very *map* of gentlemanly behavior, for you shall find in him the *continent* of whatever part a gentleman would see."

After rolling his eyes for Horatio's entertainment, Hamlet returned, "Sir, his description suffers no loss in you; though I know to catalogue him would dizzy the arithmetic of memory, and yet would sway erratically for all that, compared to his quick sail. *But* ... to truly praise him, I take him to be a soul of great importance, and his quality of such scarcity and rareness as, to speak accurately of him, his likeness is his mirror ... and whoever else may follow him would be his *shadow* ... and *nothing* more."

Again, Osric seemed unsure as to how to receive the Prince's words. After a pregnant pause, he ventured, "Your lordship speaks most infallibly of him."

"Mmm ... And *how* does this concern us, sir? Why *do*

we wrap the gentleman in our unskilled, insufficient praise?"

"... sir?"

Horatio spoke up. "Is it not possible to understand in any tongue but your own? You can do it, sir, if you really try."

Hamlet chuckled, then tried again. "What imports the *naming* of this gentleman?"

"Of Laertes?"

Horatio threw his hands into the air – such a lost cause! "His purse is already empty," he commented to Hamlet, "all his golden words are spent."

To Osric, Hamlet confirmed, "Of *him*, sir."

Cautiously, so as not to offend, Osric began, "I *know* you are not ... um, ignorant—"

"I would you did, sir ... yet, in faith, even if you did, it would not much commend me. Well, sir?"

Osric quickly offered, "You are not ignorant of what *excellence* Laertes is—"

"I dare not confess *that*, lest I should claim the same 'excellence' for myself; for to know a man well, would be to know oneself."

"I mean, sir, for his *weapon*, which by popular estimate, in his merit he stands without equal."

Genuinely intrigued for the first time in this entire conversation, Hamlet asked, "What's his weapon?"

"Rapier and dagger."

"That's *two* of his weapons – but well ..."

Speaking over Horatio's latest chortle, Osric finally found his stride. "The King, sir, has wagered with him six Barbary horses – against which he has imponed, as I take it, six French rapiers and poniards with their gear, such as girdle, straps, and so on. Three of the carriages, in faith, are very tasteful, matching well to the hilts – most delicate carriages, and of very elegant design."

"What did you call the ... 'carriages'?"

Horatio mumbled, "I knew you would require enlightenment from a glossary before you were done."

Hamlet snickered under his breath.

For his part, Osric explained, "The carriages, sir, are the *straps*."

"The phrase would be more germane to the matter, if we could carry *cannons* by our sides – I would it might be *hangers* till then. But, onward: Six Barbary horses against six French swords, their gear, and three elegantly-designed 'carriages'; that's the French bet against the Danish. Why is this all ... 'imponed,' as you call it?"

"The King, sir, has wagered, that in a dozen bouts between yourself and Laertes, he shall not exceed you by three hits. He has bet on twelve-for-nine; and it would come to immediate trial, if your lordship would vouchsafe the answer."

Hamlet considered this for a moment. "What if I answer ... 'No'?"

Osric, too, considered his next words – clearly, the thought that the Prince might decline this challenge had never crossed his little mind. "I mean, my lord, the opposition of your person in trial."

Hamlet smiled, and sauntered over to the young courtier. "Sir, I will walk here in the hall: If it pleases his majesty, it is my time for exercise. Let the foils be brought, the gentleman willing, and if the King holds his purpose, I consent to win for him ... and I *can*. If not, I will gain nothing but my shame, and the odd hits."

Osric was pleased and relieved. "Shall I redeliver you even so?"

"To this effect, sir: With whatever embellishment you desire."

Osric bowed dramatically. "I offer my respects to your lordship."

"Yours, yours."

Osric offered one more, unnecessary bow, slipped his hat back onto his head, performed a pseudo-military about-face, and departed.

"He does well to commend it himself; there are no other tongues to do it for him," Hamlet commented.

"This foolish bird runs away almost before he is hatched."

Hamlet snorted his derision. "He paid courtesy to his mother's nipple before he sucked it. Thus has he – and many more of the same breed that I know the frivolous age dotes on – got only fashionable speech and superficial mannerisms; a kind of frothy collection of phrases, which allows them to hold their own amidst the most profound judgments – if you blow on them, their bubbles are blown away."

Horatio opened his mouth to speak, to turn the topic away from Osric and toward the far more alarming prospect of his friend's fencing against the known skill of Laertes. Before he could begin, however, the door through which Osric had retreated opened once more, and a more seasoned lord entered. He, too, came to attention before his Prince, though with much less rigidity.

"My lord, his majesty commended him to you by young Osric, who brings back to him the news that you will attend him in the hall. He sends me to learn if your pleasure holds to play with Laertes, or that you will require longer time."

Hamlet shrugged with precise apathy. "I am constant to my purpose; they follow the King's pleasure – if the time is good for him, it is good for me; now or whensoever, provided I am as able as I am now."

"The King and Queen and all are coming down."

This surprised Hamlet somewhat, though he kept his features neutral. Why the sudden hurry for a match against Laertes? What was Claudius up to now? To the lord, he simply said, "An opportune time."

"The Queen desires you to offer some courteous greeting to Laertes before you fall to play."

"She instructs me well."

With that, the lord seemed satisfied that he had covered all aspects of their exchange. He bowed slightly, and left.

In a low, concerned voice, Horatio said, "You will *lose* this wager, my lord."

Hamlet waved that away. "I do not think so. Since Laertes went to France, I have been in continual practice – I shall win the three hits." He suddenly seemed very tired. "Still ... you would not think how ill all's here about my heart ... but it is no matter."

"*No*, my good lord—"

"It is but foolery; but it is such a kind of misgiving, as would perhaps trouble a woman."

"If your mind dislikes *any*thing, obey it! I will forestall their arrival here, and say you are not fit."

But Hamlet again waved it away. He returned to the couch, and Horatio joined him as Hamlet said, "Not a whit, we defy an omen." He smiled without humor, and cited

Matthew 10:29: "There's a special providence in the fall of a sparrow."

Horatio was clearly unsettled by this Biblical reference, and Hamlet turned so that he could address his friend directly.

"If death is now, it is not to come; if death is *not* to come, it will be now. And ... if it is *not* now, then death *will* come. Only the *readiness* is everything. Since no man knows anything of anything he leaves behind ... what is it to leave early?" He touched his friend's shoulder. "*Enough*."

Perhaps Hamlet was trying to offer Horatio comfort, perhaps not.

Regardless, Horatio blinked away the tears.

*　　*　　*

Less than an hour later, Horatio stood alongside his Prince in the great hall, the room of state at Elsinore, where he had first found Hamlet upon his return to Denmark.

Quite a crowd had gathered. Considering that there was nothing "official" about this event, a disproportionate number of nobles, lords, and courtiers made up the audience – rounded out by a healthy number of attendants, of course. A long, narrow, black-and-white striped carpet had been laid down parallel to the dais, its center directly across from the throne. A table had also been set up on the opposite side, upon which lay a number of swords from which the contestants would select their weapons.

Hamlet and Laertes had arrived wearing the heavy canvas coats which would protect their torsos during the bout. Fencing masks were readily available, but in recent years, it had been considered somewhat ... uncouth ... to don this additional protection. There was no real logic to this trend, and if pressed, few would be able to articulate exactly *why* it was frowned upon. Perhaps it implied cowardice on the part of the wearer. Or, just as likely (and foolish), it was interpreted as an insult to one's opponent, as it suggested their skill could not be trusted, that they lacked sufficient control to safely keep their blade away from one's delicate features. After all, this was a *contest*, nothing more; the goal was not to actually *injure* the adversary ... merely to *shame* them by scoring hit after hit.

Regardless, it added entirely unnecessary risk to the match, risk that Horatio feared on behalf of his Prince ... but he knew that neither Hamlet nor Laertes would wear a mask. There was little point in even suggesting otherwise.

Hamlet stood with Horatio on one end of the strip; Laertes and his own attendant waited at the other. If death could be served with a mere glance, then Laertes would already have delivered Hamlet beyond need of mask or coat.

Finally, the King rose, and all fell silent. With Gertrude at his side, Claudius strode forward, stepping from his throne to the center of the strip. Likewise, Hamlet and Laertes approached from their respective ends, until all three parties met in the middle of the strip, and of the room.

Claudius took Laertes' waiting hand, then turned to address his nephew. "Come, Hamlet, come, and take this hand from me."

After a moment's hesitation – a moment so brief that few in the audience even perceived it – Hamlet obeyed. Under Claudius' guidance, Hamlet and Laertes found themselves clasping hands.

Normally, the opponents would share this grasp for a moment or two, and then part. But, to the surprise of everyone present, Hamlet held on to Laertes a bit longer. In a low voice, he said, "Give me your pardon, sir: I've done you wrong; but pardon it, as you are a gentleman. This August assembly knows, and you must have heard, how I am afflicted with sore distraction. What I have done – that might roughly awaken your feelings of honor and disapproval – I hereby proclaim was *madness*. Was it *Hamlet* who wronged Laertes? No, *not* Hamlet: If Hamlet is taken away from himself, and when he's not himself does wrong to Laertes ... then Hamlet does not do it, Hamlet *denies* it." He paused, glanced away from Laertes' still-burning gaze. "*Who* does it, then? His madness: If it is so, Hamlet is of the faction that is wronged; his madness is poor Hamlet's enemy." Now he looked back, meeting Laertes' eyes fully, and raised his voice so that everyone could hear, "Sir, in this audience, let my renouncing an evil purpose *free* me so far in your most generous thoughts, that I have shot my arrow over the house ... and hurt my *brother*."

Silence followed. Heavy, tense silence. Many present had been *displeased*, to put it mildly, by Hamlet's recent abhorrent behavior. But this apology and appeal for Laertes' forgiveness sounded heartfelt and sincere, and everyone waited to see how Laertes would respond.

When at last he spoke, his voice was flat and came through clenched teeth. "I am ... *satisfied* in my personal feeling – whose motive, in this case, should stir me to my revenge. But in my terms of *honor* ... I stand aloof; and will not reconcile, till by some elder masters, of known honor, I have a public opinion and precedent of peace, to keep my name unmarred. But ... till that time, I do receive your offered love *like* love ... and will not wrong it."

Hamlet smiled and gave Laertes' hand one final shake before releasing it. "I embrace it freely; and will play this amicable wager freely." He clapped his hands together, and called out with mock severity, "Give us the foils! Come on!"

"Come, one for me," Laertes agreed.

The audience's collective breath relaxed as the two continued to banter about in a manner that was at least *somewhat* playful.

"I'll be your shining foil, Laertes," Hamlet returned, "in my ignorance, *your* skill shall indeed blaze like a star in the darkest night."

"You mock me, sir."

"No, by this hand."

Chuckling, Claudius called out, "Give them the foils, young Osric." As the two men sauntered over to the weapons table, he continued in his boisterous voice, "Cousin Hamlet, you know the wager?"

"Very well, my lord. Your grace has wagered a greater stake on the weaker side."

Claudius scoffed, which pleased Gertrude. "I do not fear it; I have seen you both – but since he has perfected his skills, we therefore *have* odds in our favor."

Ignoring their exchange, Laertes was already busy selecting his blade. "This is too heavy," he grumbled at Osric, "let me see another."

By contrast, Hamlet was quite cheery. "*This* one pleases me well. These foils have all the same length?"

"Aye, my good lord," Osric assured him.

Finally, having each chosen their preferred blade, the

contestants stepped onto the fencing strip.

Snapping his fingers, Claudius commanded, "Set the tankards of wine upon that table. If Hamlet gives the first or second hit, or retaliates against Laertes' two hits in the third exchange, let all the battlements fire their ordnance! The King shall drink to Hamlet's renewed energy; and into the cup ..." He reached into a fold near his wrist, and held what he withdrew high for all to see. "... I shall throw a *pearl* of the finest quality, richer than that which four successive kings in Denmark's crown have worn. Give me the cups; and let the kettle-drum speak to the trumpet, the trumpet to the cannoneer without, the cannons to the heavens, the heavens to earth, 'Now the King drinks to Hamlet!'"

With this, he stepped back to his throne, and his wife followed suit. "Come, begin!" he cheered. "And you, the judges, bear a wary eye!"

The contestants stepped forward, saluting one another before slipping into their respective opening postures.

"Come on, sir," Hamlet said, so softly that it did not carry beyond the strip.

"Come, my lord," Laertes replied in a bolder voice.

The King raised his hand high in the air, held it aloft for a scant heartbeat, then brought it down swiftly.

The game was on.

Both men exploded into action, and as a result, each was nearly struck by the other as they failed to form mutual defense in time. Then it was Laertes pressing forward, edging Hamlet back, back ...

... back to the end of the strip, where the Prince feigned slipping to one knee. Laertes lunged in for the kill, only to find Hamlet's foil stabbing a sharp ache into his arm pit.

"One!" Hamlet cried.

"No!" Laertes seethed.

Laughing, Hamlet called out. "Judgement!"

"A *hit*!" Osric announced for the Prince, the challenger, and all the audience. "A very *palpable* hit!"

Hamlet laughed once more, and it was almost too much for Laertes. As the Prince turned to bow toward his applauding mother, he summoned his deepest reserves of strength to avoid skewering the murderer through the back of the skull then and there.

An accident, he reminded himself with force. *The King wishes it to appear as an* accident.

And so, gritting his teeth so fiercely it made his jaws ache, he muttered, "Well ... again."

King Claudius, for his part, hooting with pleasure that bordered on overzealous. "Stay; give me drink!" An attendant rushed to provide the goblet. "Hamlet, this pearl is yours; here's to your health."

As Claudius drank deeply, the trumpets sounded and cannons fired, as ordered. The King held the great pearl high for all to glimpse one last time, then dropped it into the goblet, into the rest of the wine.

Ah, Laertes noted with silent satisfaction.

Handing the tainted chalice back to the attendant, Claudius gleefully commanded, "Give him the cup."

But Hamlet held up a dismissive hand. "I'll play this bout first; set it by awhile." This brought both Claudius and Laertes a chill of unpleasant surprise, but before they could so much as share a meaningful glance, Hamlet called, "Come!"

The fencing resumed. As before, it appeared that the

much-touted skill of Laertes would prove triumphant, but as before, Hamlet's cunning got the better of him. This time the Prince caught him unprepared by passing him completely and scoring a touch in his blind spot.

"Another hit; what do you say?" he smirked.

Laertes felt as though his teeth would be ground to powder before this day was over. "A touch," he growled, "a touch, I do confess."

Ever the better actor of the conspirators, Claudius appeared sincere as he turned to his wife and announced, "Our son shall win."

Gertrude, for her part, was absolutely beaming. She rose to her feet as she replied, "He's sweaty, and scant of breath."

Claudius tensed as she scooped up the Prince's laced goblet and strode toward her son, but then he allowed himself a private smile. How perfect! The Queen herself would dispose of this matter *for* him, once and for all.

"Here, Hamlet," she said as she reached her son and offered her handkerchief, "take my napkin, rub your brows."

Grinning like a fool to Claudius' eyes, Hamlet accepted the cloth.

Then Gertrude ...

Then Gertrude turned and, holding the poisoned wine high, called out, "The Queen toasts your fortune, Hamlet."

"Good madam," her son replied as he loosened his protective tunic to dab at the sweat on the back of his neck.

Gertrude held the wine higher still, then brought the cup to her lips.

Claudius was on his feet, his heart threatening to hammer straight through his ribs. "*Gertrude!*" he cried.

Fortunately, she froze, the cup still an inch from her mouth.

*Un*fortunately, *everyone* froze ... and stared. The Queen, her damnable son, Osric, the guards, the courtiers, and especially the gaping Laertes.

What could he say? *Don't drink that evil potion, my love, for it was intended to kill the threat that is your son, Hamlet, the Prince of Denmark.* No. There was nothing he could say that would not immediately reveal him for what he was – a scheming murderer.

But still he stood, and still they stared. Finally, awkwardly, he said merely, "Do not drink." And nothing else.

Understandably mystified, Gertrude merely shook her head in befuddlement. "I *will*, my lord; I pray you, pardon me."

Repeated her gesture of praise ... and drank.

It is the poisoned cup! Claudius so wanted to scream. And he truly did want to. Whatever his faults, whatever his *motives* in marrying this doomed woman, he truly loved her. Just ... not enough to expose himself. Was that so wrong?

But then, it did not matter.

It is too late.

In the meantime, Gertrude had finished her small but deadly swallow and offered the cup to Hamlet. "I dare not drink yet, madam," he declined, still mopping away at the back of his neck, "by and by."

Handing the cup off to one of her aides, she laughed and took the handkerchief from him. "Come, let *me* wipe your face." She helped him open his tunic a touch further so that his hot skin could breathe at the throat, then proceeded to pamper and blot his features.

All the while, Laertes had edged himself closer to the King. "My lord," he whispered, "I'll hit him now."

The King returned, through numb lips, "I do not think so," as though he no longer cared whether Laertes would be able to strike with the poisoned blade or not. He then turned his back on the younger man and shuffled back to his throne.

Laertes, too, returned to his post on the strip, and his eyes followed the Queen as she joined her husband. *And yet, it is almost against my conscience.*

All grin, not even bothering to re-tighten his tunic, Hamlet slashed his blade across the air and called, "Come, for the third, Laertes – you only dally. I pray you: Pass with your best violence; I am afraid you are holding back to *let* me win!"

Whatever hesitation Laertes had begun to feel evaporated with the taunt. "Say you so?" He slashed his own blade in mock fashion. "Come on!"

When they crossed swords this time, Laertes offered more of his anticipated muster. Hamlet tried another trick or two, but they failed on this go. They lunged, parried, lunged, parried, until finally they both lunged at the same time, missing each other in blades but colliding in body. They tipped, and it appeared that they would both fall. Instead, both men got their balance, but it cost each of them a foot off the strip.

At her throne, Gertrude grunted, then cleared her throat.

"Nothing," Osric judged, "neither way."

Smirking and mugging for the crowd, Hamlet held his hands out before him as though to say, *Oh, well, what is one to do?*

Gertrude laughed, but it quickly evolved into a cough. At this, Claudius placed a hand over his mouth to stifle a soft moan.

Laertes, however, had forgotten the dismal fate of the Queen. He was watching Hamlet, watching the exposed skin at the nape of his neck. Watching him turn, watching him exchange looks with Horatio...

What if the match continued thus? What if Hamlet's surprising and upsetting skill fended him off before he could score a blow – not "just" a blow, but one firm enough to bite through the protection of his fencing tunic – and therefore infest him with the poison?

Laertes would not have it.

Hamlet was returning to his end of the strip, and Laertes advanced upon him, first silently then with emphasis on speed.

"Have at you now!"

He lashed out, and his blade scratched across the back of Hamlet's neck down toward his left shoulder. The Prince whirled, far more shocked than pained. The audience gasped.

Laertes smirked at him, his secret knowledge of the Prince's short-lived destiny making him smug.

And Hamlet exploded.

Bellowing like a crazed animal, he charged. But it wasn't a "lunge" or an "offense" in any civilized meaning of the word. It was *an attack*. He swung his sword with one hand and threw punches with the other. All the anger, all the confusion, all the sorrow he'd experienced in recent months erupted to the surface as he finally – *finally* – found a concrete, *accessible* focus for his rage.

Laertes was unable to defend himself. His sword prevented any mortal slashes, but his cheek, his forearm, and his thigh bled, as did his nose from Hamlet's hooking fist.

The King and Queen were on their feet, although Gertrude rose too fast and dizziness forced her back down. She tried to call out to her son, but this only caused another coughing fit. Why did her throat burn so ...?

Finally, Hamlet brought his blade down on the wrist of Laertes' sword hand. This disarmed him, but it struck so hard that Hamlet, too, lost his weapon. He reached down, grabbing the first sword he found.

Laertes' eyes widened in terror – Hamlet had grabbed the wrong sword; *his* sword; the *poisoned* sword!

"Part them!" the King commanded to everyone and no one. "They are incensed!"

"*Nay!*" Hamlet raged. He turned on Laertes once more. "Come, again!"

But Laertes had no interest in crossing swords with Hamlet again – especially not crossing *that* sword. He turned and fled, with Hamlet in hot pursuit.

Laertes reached as far as the common soldiers, who had gathered to view this great contest. And he found, much to his misfortune, that they did not favor this unexplained, unexpected, *unwanted* show of great cowardice. They did not part for him.

And then Hamlet was upon him.

The blade bit into the lower of Laertes' back.

Laertes cried out. Literally. *Cried* out, with far more feeling than equaled the actual pain he experienced. Not to suggest that the blade did not sink *deep* – oh, yes, it did. Even if it were not for the poison, he felt something tear inside ...

Hamlet withdrew the sword, and drew back for another attack ...

... and that's when the Queen collapsed to the floor before her throne.

Osric noticed first. "Look to the Queen there, ho!"

Horatio appeared in the chaos, seizing his friend. But Hamlet did not fight back – he was staring across the room at this mother. "They bleed on *both* sides," Horatio spat at Osric and the other judges with heavy distaste. "How is it, my lord?"

Osric leaned over Laertes, who had remained on the floor where he had fallen under Hamlet's assault. Under the circumstances, he would have expected the man to rise again and further retreat from the crazed Prince. And yet ... he did not. "How is it, Laertes?"

Laertes surprised him by actually laughing in response ... a laugh which very swiftly ran to tears. "Why, as a woodcock to my own spring, Osric," he finally answered in a low voice. "I am justly killed with my own treachery."

Hamlet, however, was no longer listening. He was still staring at the swarm of attendants and aides who had gathered around his ailing mother. She was now coughing so hard that it seemed she would soon break something within her chest. "How is the Queen?!"

Much to his gall, it was Claudius who answered, "She ... she swoons to see them bleed!"

Upon hearing this falsehood, Gertrude came alive, in a manner of speaking. She shoved away the closest of her attendants and forced herself to stop coughing through sheer force of will. In a dry, cracking, pained voice, she made herself heard by all. "No, *no*, the drink, the drink! Oh, my dear, Hamlet ... the drink, *the drink*! I ... am ... *poisoned*."

With that, she collapsed, and this time her coughing *did* break something inside. Blood oozed from her mouth, her nose, even – it seemed – her eyes. Her breath rattled loudly in her chest one final time ... and she died.

For a few seconds, all were silent. Then Hamlet, as his mother before him, "came alive." He shrugged away Horatio, who did not resist, and ordered, "Oh, villainy! Ho! Let the doors be locked!" Several guards rushed to obey. "Treachery! Seek it out!"

"It is *here*, Hamlet!"

The Prince turned to gape at the unlikely source of the declaration.

Still lying on the floor, his own words now punctuated by the occasional cough, Laertes continued, "Hamlet ... you are slain; no medicine in the world can do you any good. There is not half an hour of life left in you. The treacherous instrument is in your hand ..."

Not quite stunned, Hamlet glanced down at Laertes' sword, which he still held.

" ... left sharpened and envenomed ... the vile plot has turned itself on *me* ... lo, here I lie, never to rise again." This time he coughed hard enough to force a longer pause. Then, "Your mother's poisoned ... I can conspire no more." In clear pain, he rolled in his position just enough to allow him to point an incriminating finger. "The King ... *the King's to blame*!"

All eyes turned.

Claudius retreated one step, then another. But he was too *overwhelmed* to simply turn and run, fleet of foot.

Not so for Hamlet.

For each step Claudius managed, Hamlet matched him with four. He was running, sprinting, descending upon his enemy.

At long last.

"The point!" he cried, wielding the sword before him. "Envenomed, too! Then, venom, *to your work*!"

He closed the final gap, and lunged. The sword bit into Claudius just above his navel, skewering him through until the tip emerged at the small of his back. He screamed.

Cries of "Treason! Treason!" echoed through the room of state. Perhaps they alluded to Hamlet's actions; perhaps they condemned Claudius'. Regardless, the reigning King took them as a sign that he had *some* followers remaining in the throng.

"Oh, yet defend me, friends!" he pleaded, his hands clutched around the blade in his belly. "I am ... but hurt!"

Hovering over him, Hamlet moved to withdraw the blade and stab a second wound. But then his eyes lit upon the goblet from which his mother drank – the goblet with the pearl, intended for *him*. Barking an unpleasant laugh, he shifted to the side and seized the cup.

Then he was poised over the throne, fairly straddling the King as he shoved the cup against his mouth hard enough to crack Claudius' front teeth.

"*Here*, you incestuous ..." Shove. "... murderous ..." Shove, the wine pouring all over, including into the King's throat. " ... *damned* Dane! *Drink* of this potion! Is your union *here*?!"

The pearl rolled forward through the last of the wine, *clacking* against the remains of Claudius' teeth. Hamlet seized it ...

... and shoved into deep into the King's right eye.

"*Follow my mother!*"

But Claudius did not react, did not respond.

The King of Denmark was dead.

"He is justly served," Laertes croaked. "It is a poison mixed by himself." He again strained to extend a hand – not to point this time, but to reach for Hamlet in penitence. "Exchange forgiveness with me, noble Hamlet ..." Cough, cough. " ... mine and my father's death come not upon you ... nor yours upon me ..."

And Laertes breathed his last.

"Heaven absolve you," Hamlet said to the corpse, before experiencing his first tightening of the throat. He indulged the cough, then brushed his fingertips across the back of his wounded neck, regarding the blood he found with something close to apathy. "I follow you."

He looked around at the amazed, stunned crowd. Finding his friend, he showed the blood to him. "I am dead, Horatio." Stumbling slightly on shaky legs, he stepped forward – away from the throne and toward his mother. "Wretched Queen ... adieu!"

Now he regarded the stupefied audience around him as he moved to meet Horatio not far from the center on the fencing strip. "You that look pale and tremble at this chance, that are but silent spectators to this act ... had I but time – as this cruel sergeant, Death, is strict in his arrest ... oh, I could tell you—"

He was caught short by another wave of coughing, this one far more violent. He lurched and started to fall, but Horatio was there to catch him and lowered him softly. The poisoned cup, which he still held tightly, very nearly spilt its final contents. " ... but let it be." He regarded his friend, who was now in tears. "Horatio, *I* am dead ... y*ou* live. Report me and my cause ... accurately to the unsatisfied."

Horatio shook his head in misery. "Never believe it. Faced with this, I am more a suicidal Roman than a Dane ..." Reaching down, Horatio attempted to pull the goblet from Hamlet's clenched hand. "There's some liquor left yet."

Hamlet might have been weakening, but he kept his hold on the poison. "As you are a *man*, give me the cup." A brief but fierce tug-of-war ensued. "Let go! By Heaven, I'll *have* it!" At last, the point became moot, as the final sips of wine splattered down onto Hamlet's tunic and lap.

Horatio released the cup, and sobbed so hard his shoulders shook.

"Oh, good Horatio ... what a wounded name – things standing thus unknown – shall live behind me!" He coughed, a harsh, ripping sound. Then, "If you ever did hold me in your heart ... excuse yourself from felicity awhile ... and, in this harsh world, draw your breath in pain ... to *tell my story*."

Horatio had appropriated some control over his weeping now, and opened his mouth to reply. Whatever he might have said was lost, however, when there suddenly arose the startled cries of men under siege. Metal on metal, the wails of the wounded, the sound of sudden and unexpected pitched battle echoing through the halls surrounding the room of state. Finally, the courtiers and guards alike cried out as a cannon erupted somewhere nearby.

"What warlike noise is this ...?" Hamlet managed through coughs.

A pale Osric stepped away from the window from which he had rushed. He answered his Prince – now King? – with a shaky and uncertain voice. "Young Fortinbras, with conquest come from Poland, gives this warlike volley to the ambassadors ... of *England*."

Hamlet considered this baffling new development for a moment, until another coughing fit reminded him that, whatever was happening outside, it was no longer his concern. He waved it away and returned his rickety focus to his friend.

"Oh ... I *die*, Horatio. The potent poison triumphs over my spirit ... I cannot live to hear the news from England ... but I do foresee the election lights on Fortinbras. *He* has my dying vote ... so tell him of the occurrences which, more and less, have instigated all of this." He coughed loud, hard ... and then seemed to find comfort. "The rest ... is ... *silence*."

And Hamlet, the Prince of Denmark, died.

For a time, Horatio simply stared down at him. The audience, who had been on the verge of breaking up until they heard the sounds of combat from without, remained still and respectful.

Finally, Horatio spoke. "Now cracks a noble heart. Good night, sweet Prince. And flights of angels sing you to your rest."

The sound of marching had been intermixed with the combat for some minutes now. A small parade, accompanied by a pacing-drumbeat, drew quite near. The largest doors – locked upon Hamlet's orders when the Queen fell – were being forced open.

"Why does the drum come here?" Horatio asked.

In short order, the doors gave way. The audience

withdrew from the bodyguards who entered first, which gave plenty of space for Prince Fortinbras and his guests from England to emerge in grand style.

All of their formidable, royal airs evaporated, however, when they laid their eyes upon the death and mayhem that awaited them within.

The English ambassadors were speechless. Fortinbras himself managed to ask, "What *is* this sight?"

"What is it you would see?" Horatio asked from where he still sat with his Prince lying in his lap. "If nothing but woe or calamity ... cease your search."

Fortinbras barely heard him. He was staring at the deceased. The King. The Queen. The Prince. Another he did not know. *What* happened here?! "This heap of bodies proclaims a massacre. Oh, proud Death, what feast is in preparation in your eternal cell, that you have so bloodily struck down so many princes at a shot?"

Finally finding some compunction – and his voice – the head Ambassador stepped forward alongside Fortinbras. "The sight is dismal; and our affairs from England come too late." He looked over at Claudius. "The ears are senseless that should give us hearing, to tell him his commandment is fulfilled, that Rosencrantz and Guildenstern are dead. Where should we have our thanks?"

Horatio breathed a sad chuckle. "Not from the *King's* mouth, had it the ability of life to thank you: *He* never gave commandment for their death. But since you so jump upon this bloody question – you from the Polack wars, and you from England – are here arrived, give order that these bodies be placed high on a platform to the view. And let me speak to the yet unknowing world how these things came about:

So shall you hear of carnal, bloody, and unnatural acts, of accidental retributions, chance slaughters, of deaths instigated by cunning and unreal cause ... and, in this upshot, purposes mistook fallen on the inventors' heads." He glanced once more upon his Prince, his friend. "All this ... I can truly deliver."

Fortinbras nodded firmly. "Let us *haste* to hear it, and call the noblest to the audience. For me ... I embrace my fortune with sorrow – I have some rights unforgotten in this kingdom, which now my ... *opportunity* ... invites me to claim."

Horatio, too, nodded. "Of that I shall also have cause to speak, and from this Prince's mouth, whose vote will draw on *more* support; but let this be performed at once, even while men's minds are distraught; lest *more* mischance on plots and errors happen."

Fortinbras clapped his hands in sharp command. His bodyguard immediately came to attention. "Let four captains bear Hamlet, like a soldier, to the platform; for he was likely, had he been put to the test, to have proved *most* royally – and, for his death, the soldiers' music and the rites of war speak loudly for him." He raised his voice higher. "Take up the bodies. Such a sight as this befits the field of battle, but in this place feels very much amiss. Go, bid the soldiers *shoot*."

The bodyguards separated, some remaining with their liege, the others rushing to bear away the deceased – most notably and carefully, Hamlet.

Horatio remained and stared after them long after they were gone. It would be some time before he could accept and appreciate the fullness of this tragedy of Denmark.

Hamlet had asked that he spread the word, that he tell the tale. And he would ... though he was not yet certain exactly *how*.

Perhaps he would seek out the Players once more.

Outside, though the combat had previously ceased, cannons were again fired. This time, they did not serve the victory of Poland.

This time, they honored the fallen Prince of Denmark.

The following literature and films were *invaluable* in my efforts to novelize *Hamlet*:

LITERATURE

The Riverside Shakespeare, 1974 edition.*
The Yale Shakespeare, 1966 edition.*
The Arden Shakespeare, 2000 edition.
Rosencrantz & Guildenstern Are Dead, by Tom Stoppard.
Asimov's Guide to Shakespeare, by Isaac Asimov.

FILMS

HAMLET

1996 version
Directed by Kenneth Branagh, starring Kenneth Branagh.

1990 version
Directed by Franco Zeffirelli, starring Mel Gibson.

1969 version
Directed by Tony Richardson, starring Nicol Williamson.

1948 version
Directed by Laurence Olivier, starring Laurence Olivier.